Fergus Hume

The Harlequin Opal

Vol. 3

Fergus Hume

The Harlequin Opal
Vol. 3

ISBN/EAN: 9783337346720

Printed in Europe, USA, Canada, Australia, Japan

Cover: Foto ©Andreas Hilbeck / pixelio.de

More available books at **www.hansebooks.com**

THE

HARLEQUIN OPAL

A ROMANCE

BY

FERGUS HUME

Author of " The Island of Fantasy," " Aladdin in London," etc.

VOLUME III

Once a realm of Indian glory,
Famed in Aztec song and story,
Fabled by Tradition hoary
　　As an earthly Paradise ;
Now a land of love romances,
Serenades, bolero dances,
Looks of scorn, adoring glances,
　　Under burning tropic skies.

LONDON

W. H. ALLEN & CO., LIMITED

13, WATERLOO PLACE, S.W.

1893

PROEM.

The stone had its birth in the nurturing earth,
  Its home in the heart of the main,
From the coraline caves it was tossed by the waves
  On the breast of an aureat plain ;
And the spirits who dwell in the nethermost hell
  Stored fire in its bosom of white ;
The sylphs of the air made it gracious and fair
  With the blue of the firmament's height.

The dull gnomes I ween, gave it glittering sheen,
  Till yellow as gold it became ;
The nymphs of the sea made the opal to be
  A beacon of emerald flame.

The many tints glow, they come and they go
  At bidding of spirits abhorr'd,
When one ray is bright, in the bosom of white,
  Its hue tells the fate of its lord.
For yellow hints wealth, and blue meaneth health,
  While green forbodes passing of gloom,
But beware of the red, 'tis an omen of dread,
  Portending disaster and doom.

INDEX.

THE HARLEQUIN OPAL.

CHAPTER I.

WITHIN THE WALLS.

Circle of stone,
Circle of steel,
Loyalists true,
Pent up in battle belts twain ;
Yet we, alone,
Doubly feel,
That with our few,
We shall a victory gain.

Climb up our foes,
Over the wall,
Deep bit the swords,
Fiercely the cannon spout fire ;
Yet 'neath our blows,
Downward they fall,
Traitorous hordes,
In torment and blood to expire.

TIM at once took his friends to his quarters, and made them comfortable, but scarcely had they finished a hurried meal, when an aide-de-camp arrived from

General Gigedo requiring their presence without delay. As Peter had received a nasty blow on the head during the *mêlée*, Jack insisted that he should remain behind and rest himself. Peter feebly remonstrated against this arrangement, as he wanted to accompany his friends, but in the end was forced to yield to their insistence. Then Duval buckled on his sword, slipped his revolvers into his belt, and went off with Tim to report himself at head-quarters.

Both of them were terribly alarmed about Philip. In the first burst of emotion Jack had deemed his friend dead ; but, on looking at the matter calmly, it seemed probable that he would yet turn up well and unhurt. It was impossible that Indians, in whatever number, could utterly exterminate a body of disciplined troops amounting to a thousand men. Tim's opinion was that if they had been attacked and overpowered by strategy, they had fled to the nearest town for shelter. As he had marched overland with Colonel Garibay from Tlatonac, he knew the country better than did Jack, and proceeded to defend his theory of the reinforcements' safety, by describing the position of the towns.

"It's a hundred miles or more as the crow flies from Tlatonac to this God-forsaken place. Within that limit are four towns, no less—one every twenty miles. When we marched south two weeks ago, we first went to Chichimec, then to Puebla de los Naranjos, which last one is midway. Hermanita is next, and then after dropping in at Centeotl, we came on to Janjalla!"

"Still, if the Indians surprised them by night they might have surrounded and exterminated the whole lot. To my mind nothing is so dangerous as a despised enemy."

"What!" cried Tim, with great contempt, "d'you mean to tell me that a lot of naked savages could manage that. By my soul, 'tis impossible!"

"But, my dear fellow, the Indians are out in thousands. Cocom told me so."

"They may be out in millions," retorted Tim, emphatically. "I tell you, Jack, they couldn't have killed all these men. A good number of them must have escaped to the nearest town, and, I'll lay my soul on it, that among those who got away is Philip. He wasn't born to be murdered by a lot of howling savages."

"Well, let us hope so," replied Jack, who was beginning to take this comfortable view of things himself; "but, tell me, Tim, when the reinforcements didn't arrive, why did you not wire to Tlatonac?"

"Begad! I couldn't. The rebels cut the telegraph wires some days since. The last message was that you and Doña Dolores had come back safely. Ah, my boy," cried Tim, slapping Jack on the the shoulder, "didn't I sing 'Glory Hallelujah,' when I heard that same. But, I knew you'd turn up again all safe."

"I didn't know it myself!" replied Jack, grimly "it was touch and go, I can tell you."

"Dioul! You must tell me all about it. But hold your noise, Jack, and don't be lamenting for Philip If you returned, so will he."

"I fervently hope so," said Jack, gloomily; "but I own that I feel doubtful. Are the wires cut on both sides of the town?"

"No! glory be to the saints. I can still telegraph to England by the wires going south, but I expect them to be cut every minute, so I'm hard at work sending all the news I can."

" Did you see the fight last night ? "

" Did I not! Whow, my boy! I guessed what was up, but till the dawn we weren't quite sure of the trouble. Begad! *The Pizarro's* gone anyhow."

" Yes. But the other warships and transports are due to-night."

" Then we'll have another fight," said Tim, coolly ; " wasn't I wishing I was on board a torpedera ! There's a heap to talk about, Jack ; how you escaped from that infernal Xuarez, and how you sank *The Pizarro*. I want to wire about that same right away."

" First I must see what the General desires. Oh, here is Garibay. A thousand greetings, Colonel."

" What, Señor Juan ! Ah, mi amigo, how pleased I am to see you safe once more. I deemed you were dead."

" Dios ! He is a merry corpse, Señor," said Tim, turning his head. " Where's the General ? "

" Within yonder house of the Jefe Politico. You also, Señor Corresponsal, does he desire to see."

" I am at the service of Señor Gigedo. Know you, Comandante, what he desires to speak of ? "

" It is that you will convey the glorious news of our naval victory to your gran'diario."

" Dios ! That will be done within an hour. I but waited to find out all particulars from Don Juan."

" Oh ! I can tell you everything," said Jack cheerfully, " I was on board *The Montezuma* with Don Rafael, and it was her torpedo which sank *The Pizarro*."

" Viva los Torpederas," shouted Garibay, who was greatly excited over this unexpected victory.

The cry was taken up by a chattering group of officers lounging in from off the General's headquarters, and Jack being recognized was at once surrounded by them. They were mostly young fellows, who were weary of being pent up within the walls of a surburban town, and saw in this sinking of *The Pizarro*, a chance of coming face to face with the enemy. It was all cries of Viva ! Bueno ! Gracias a Dios ! as Duval passed through their midst, and many would fain have detained him, to learn particulars of the combat; but Jack was anxious to hear Gigedo's views concerning the non-arrival of the reinforcements, so entered the mansion at once. Colonel Garibay conducted them both without delay to the General's apartments.

Gigedo, cigarette in mouth, was poring over a large map of the country, evidently tracing the line of march from Tlatonac, but on seeing Duval, he sprang up and advanced to salute him, with a pleased smile.

" A thousand congratulations, Señor, on your escape from the hands of Xuarez," he said, warmly ; " and still more on your gallant conduct of last night."

" Oh ! as to that, General, I was but an onlooker," replied Duval, modestly. " The credit of sinking *The Pizarro* rests with Don Rafael Maraquando. Have you heard the particulars ? "

" Assuredly Señor, Don Sebastian de Ahumada has left me but this moment. He informed me of the affair, and also delivered the instructions from His Excellency. I find here," added Gigedo, striking a pile of papers with his open hand, " that over a thousand men left Tlatonac for the front, four days ago."

" That is so, General. My friend, Señor Felipe, was with them."

" They have not arrived, Don Juan. The troops of Xuarez cannot have intercepted them and I am at a loss to understand this delay. Can you explain ? "

"Señor," said Jack after a pause, "before I left Tlatonac there were rumours of an Indian rising. While a prisoner at Totatzine I saw myself the tribes, incited to war by Ixtlilxochitli, the High Priest of the Chalchuih Tlatonac."

"Ah, that cursed opal!" cried Garibay, fiercely; "it is the cause of great trouble. Would that it could be taken from the Indians."

"Rest content, Señor Garibay; it *is* taken from the Indians. Doña Dolores took it from the shrine, and it is now in Tlatonac."

"Dios!" exclaimed the General and Garibay, simultaneously, while Tim was scarcely less astonished.

"Naturally enough the Indians wish to recover this sacred gem, Señor, therefore the rising has taken place sooner than was expected. I fear, gentlemen, that the Indians have surprised and massacred our poor friends."

"Santissima Madre! a thousand men?"

"The Indian forces amount to three times that number," said Jack, quickly. "It is true that His Excellency, at my request, sent messengers after the reinforcements to warn them of a possible attack. Yet it is not unlikely that these messengers may have been intercepted by the Indians. They might have fallen on the reinforcements without warning, and then—Señor, three thousand against one thousand—an unexpected attack. Alas! it is a terrible risk."

"Our troops may have retreated to one of the towns," said Gigedo, taking the same view of the case as had Tim. "This I would know if the telegraph wires had not been cut. But as it is we can but wait."

"And meantime," remarked Garibay, dryly "Xuarez will land some troops—already two thousand lie before the town—we have hard work, even behind our walls to keep them back. Now we have scarcely five hundred here capable of defending the town. Many are dead and wounded—fever and dysentery prevail greatly. If Xuarez lands more troops and makes an immediate attack Janjalla must fall."

"He cannot land more troops while *The Iturbide* and the torpederas guard the harbour." said Gigedo in a tone of some displeasure ; "and even if these two thousand again assault the walls we can hold out until reinforcements arrive. His Excellency tells me that two thousand men are to follow in ten days."

"Hark !" cried Tim, as Garibay was about to reply ; "a gun !—another. Señores, the war-ships are at it again. With your permission, General."

He hastily left the room and went off to the walls where he was soon afterwards joined by Jack, who had been hurriedly dismissed by the General. They looked seaward, and saw the performance of a most extraordinary drama.

It was now about three o'clock, and the ocean like a sheet of glass stretched in an inclined plane upward to the distant horizon. Owing to the elevation of the city walls they looked down, as from the heights of an amphitheatre. The ramparts were crowded with spectators, townsfolk and soldiers. Immediately below was the beach, the rebel camp—then the long pier shooting out into the blue, and beyond the flashing expanse of the sea. *The Iturbide* was lying a quarter of a mile from the shore with her two torpederas, one on each side of her. The cruiser had swung round, and was firing her guns at a slowly approaching warship.

"*The Columbus!*" cried Jack, when his eyes fell upon this vessel.

"True for you, John," said Tim, handing him the glass. "She has come south by herself. I thought you told me the transports were not due here till midnight."

"No more they are. I expect Xuarez, learning through his spies of our departure from Tlatonac has sent *The Columbus* on ahead to join forces with *The Pizarro*. With two warships he hopes to keep our lot at bay till the transports with the *Cortes* are safe in the harbour."

"The sinking of *The Pizarro* will rather upset his plans. *The Columbus* dare not attack two torpederas and a cruiser, single-handed."

"Upon my soul! that seems exactly what she intends to do, Tim."

A low murmur of surprise arose from the crowd on the ramparts, who were eagerly watching the war-ships. It seemed as though *The Columbus* was bent on her own destruction, for she came steaming straight ahead for the three ships of the Junta, insolently flying the red flag of Xuarez.

"What the deuce does she mean," cried Tim, in perplexity. "Surely she can't mistake *The Iturbide* for her consort."

"Perhaps she intends to desert," suggested Jack.

The Columbus was now more within range, and though hitherto she had been silent under the fire of *The Iturbide*, she now began to speak in her turn, and a white line of smoke ran along her black sides as the balls came singing over the water.

"Not much deserting about that," said Tim, grimly; "no! the rebels have some scheme in their heads."

By this time Pedraza was thoroughly enraged at the insolence of this one ship attacking him single-handed, and signalled at once to the torpederas. The captain of *The Columbus* saw that the signals ordered the boats to "up anchor," and acted accordingly. In a surprisingly short space of time the rebel ship had swung round, and with full steam ahead was standing out to sea. The ships of the Junta were taken by surprise at their manœuvre, and it was fully a question of an hour before they started in pursuit. Tim shut his glass with a click.

"Jack, I see it all. *The Columbus* wants to get our boats out of the harbour so as to let *The Cortes* and the transports slip in together."

"Rather a risky game, Tim." She'll be overhauled and sunk by the torpederas in no time."

"Not while she can keep them off with her heavy guns! What speed have the torpederas?"

"Eighteen to nineteen knots."

"And *The Columbus*?"

"Well, Rafael says her ordinary speed is fifteen but in case of need she can crack up steam to eighteen."

-"Even that gives the torpederas one knot to the good. But she can outsteam *The Iturbide*."

"Oh yes; sixteen is *her* limit!"

"Then I tell you what! *The Columbus*, as I said, has come here as a decoy—she knows the cruiser can't touch her speed, and she hopes to keep the torpederas at a safe distance with her heavy guns. She's off in a bee line straight out, and the other boats are after her. Then she'll dodge them and steam back here to find *The Cortes* and the transports all safe in harbour."

" I believe you are right, Tim."

"Of course I'm right. Look at the way she's smoking through the water."

Jack put the glass to his eyes and saw *The Columbus* was travelling at top speed towards the open sea. After her scampered the two torpedo boats like hounds on her trail. Further behind *The Iturbide* with the black smoke vomiting from her funnels was putting her soul into the chase. Pedraza was evidently determined to follow up one victory by another, and over eager to sink or capture the crack ironclad of the rebels, forgot all about the incoming transports. Thus, in half an hour the four ships were mere specks on the horizon, and the harbour of Janjalla was left open for the arrival of Xuarez and fresh troops.

The crowd of people on the ramparts were too excited at the stirring spectacle of the chase to think of such a thing, and yelled themselves hoarse in cheering for Pedraza. Below on the beach the rebels, who had evidently understood the manœuvres of

The Columbus, were cheering vigorously for Don Hypolito.

"Wait you dogs," cried Jack, shaking his fists at them; "soon shall you sing another tune."

"By all the saints so shall we," said Tim, wisely: "unless the forts keep off the transports we'll have another two thousand troops down there this night, and then—it's wigs on the green there will be."

"I agree with you, Tim—unless the reinforcements arrive."

"Even then, four thousand attacking a town can do a powerful lot, and when the re-inforcements arrive we'll only have one thousand five hundred to put against them. However, let us not despair," added Tim, philosophically. "Come with me, Don Juan, and we'll look over the town. Then we'll go and see if there is any sign of the new troops."

Jack assented, and descending from the ramparts they made their way through the town to the house where Tim had his quarters. The streets were filled with soldiers, who mostly looked smart, and well fitted for their work. Here and there were wounded men, and a few sick with malarian fever from the adjacent swamp, but on the whole it was wonderful how healthy was the town. Twice had the rebels assaulted the walls and twice been beaten back, not without considerable loss of men on the side of the loyalists. Fortunately, provisions were plentiful, and it was the cool season, therefore the troops of the Junta were in comparatively good condition. Despite their small numbers, they were so heartened by the sinking of *The Pizarro*, that it was plain they would fight like fiends to hold Janjalla until aid arrived from the capital.

The townspeople took the fact of being besieged in the most contented manner, and hardly interrupted their daily occupations. In the streets the tortilleras were crying their wares, the water-carriers proclaiming the fact that they sold "aqua limpia," and, but for the unusual number of soldiers, it would have been quite impossible to see that the city was in the very jaws of danger. At times a woman wrapped in the rebozo would pass along the street, but as a rule they kept within doors, and showed themselves but rarely. In the plazas men were being drilled, and many of the houses were used as hospitals for the sick and wounded.

Tim and Jack made their way through the crowded streets, and duly arrived at the former's quarters, where they found Peter eagerly expecting them. He was weary of being by himself, and when he heard they were going to the land-gate to seek news of the reinforcements, insisted on accompanying them. After taking a drink of aguardiente, of which they stood much in need, owing to the exhaustion caused by excitement, the three friends set off at once to see if they could hear anything about the expected troops.

Don Sebastian was fraternising with the captain in command of the cavalry, as his own troops had been sent forward to the sea ramparts. The mounted regiments were stationed at this end of the town as they were more useful in sallies than were the infantry. This was proved by the way in which they had succoured the soldiers from *The Iturbide*, as only horsemen could have kept the rebel troops at bay.

" No signs yet, Señor," said Don Sebastian, politely; "but half an hour ago the general sent out two Indian scouts with instructions to inquire at Centeotl for our men."

" That is twenty miles away."

"Yes; but these Indians travel fast. Before midnight we shall hear news of our troops—that is if they get as far south as Centeotl."

"And before midnight Xuarez will have landed his new regiments," said Tim, turning away. "Well, there's no help for it, I suppose. Come, Jack and Peter,' tis no use waiting here. We must wait till these scouts return."

"And meanwhile, Tim?"

"Come with me to the telegraph-office. I'm going to send an account of the sea-fight to my paper."

"You are sure the wires are not cut to the southward?" said Peter, as they trudged along to the office.

"They weren't this morning anyhow. Why should they cut them? All they want to do is to intercept communication with the capital. They don't care two straws what goes to England."

"Xuarez does. He told me so."

"Ah! but, you see, Xuarez is not here at present, and has forgotten to give orders to cut them. When he arrives again, he'll do it, maybe."

"Well, seeing that he wishes the world to look on him as a noble patriot, he certainly won't care about your wiring plain truths about him to the old country. He'll either cut the wires or bring a war correspondent on his own hook."

" A rival!" cried Tim, indignantly. " If I thought so, I'd shoulder a musket myself, and go out to shoot the dirty villain. Here's the P.O., my boys! Peter! hold your noise. Jack's going to give me a history of the fight."

."I know as much about it as Jack does," said Peter, in an injured tone, as they entered the office.

" Then I'll let you put in a word here and there," replied his friend, in a kind tone. " Why, Peter, I'd do anything to please you. Didn't I think you were knocked out of time, entirely. Manuel, are the wires right ?"

" Yes, Señor," replied the operator, a dark alert-looking man ; " all safe to Truxillo !"

" Bueno! Then they will be safe to England. Truxillo is in Honduras, and is as right as the Bank. Come, Jack, begin at once !"

They were over two hours at this business as, what with Jack's roundabout descriptions and Peter's interruptions, it took some time for Tim to get the story ship-shape. Then Manuel was constantly wiring the intelligence, as transmitted to him by Tim, who took full advantage of the licence given by his editor to send extensive telegrams. It was close on six o'clock when he finished, and he was just stretching himself with a yawn after his long spell of sitting, when outside a murmur began. It rapidly swelled into a roar and the three friends rushed out of the office to learn what new event had taken place. The telegraph-office was situated in the street which ran straight to the land-gate, and down this street they saw advancing a dense body of men.

" Vivas los soldatos ! Viva el Republico ! "

" Hurrah ! " roared Tim, wildly, " 'tis the reinforcements ! "

" There's Philip ! " cried Jack, pushing his way through the crowd.

" And wounded ! " said Peter, noticing with a true professional eye that Cassim's left arm hung useless by his side.

The Janjalla Band, stationed in the Plaza, burst out into the patriotic strains of the " Opal Fandango," he crowd yelled and cheered, the soldiers tramped steadily down the street ; and Tim, to the imminent danger of his life, flung himself almost under the feet of Philip's horse.

"Philip, my dear boy! Here we are."

"Tim! Jack! Thank God!" cried Philip, and urging his horse a little way to the side, jumped down from the saddle.

Tim gripped one hand, Jack the other, and Peter patted the baronet on the back. Philip looked worn and haggard, and winced as Tim seized his left hand.

"Are you wounded?" cried Tim, letting it go.

"Yes; but not badly! An Indian arrow through the fleshy part of the arm."

"Ah!" exclaimed Jack, anxiously, "then Cocom was right. You have been attacked by Indians."

"Two days ago! They surprised our camp by night, and came in in overwhelming force. Velez was unable to rally his men, and we were forced to retreat to Centeotl."

"And how many men have you brought, Philip?"

"Six hundred!"

"And one thousand started from Tlatonac," said Jack, sadly; "four hundred killed. Thank God, Philip, you at least are safe."

CHAPTER II.

THE FALL OF JANJALLA.

They mount the ramparts, and they man the walls,
Resolved to keep the climbing foe at bay,
The hot-mouthed cannon hurl a thousand balls,
A thousand swords flash forth to wound and slay.
Down in the fosse the planted ladder falls,
And smoke sulphurous spreads its veil of grey;
Like incense from an altar up it rolls,
To tell the war-god that a thousand souls
Are to his honour sacrificed this day.

Oh, Mars! Oh, red Bellona! he or she,
Though fallen your shrines, we bend yet 'neath your yoke;
Born later than the Greeks, we seem to be
Not much more civilised than were those folk,
Instead of spears, and shields, and cutlery,
Revolvers, rifles, guns, spit fire and smoke.
For ye, blood-thirsty pair, we yet retain
Our ancient love, and hence on battle plain
With myriad victims we your names invoke.

THE siege of Janjalla lasted five days, and during that period the town was completely invested by the troops of Xuarez. As had been foreseen by him, the *Columbus*, acting as a decoy, had drawn away the ships of the Junta from protecting the harbour, and that same night Xuarez, under cover of darkness, landed four thousand troops from his transports. By an inconceivable oversight on the part of the engineers, the city walls were unprovided with search-lights and electric apparatus, so Don Hypolito was enabled to land boat-load after boat-load of men without hindrance. By dawn six thousand men were encamped on the beach, under the very guns of the forts.

Had Xuarez attacked the capital, he would have been easily repulsed, for in Tlatonac all the latest inventions for defence were to be found. Krupp's guns pointed from the forts, powerful electric lights swept the harbour, and the bed of the ocean in front of the sea-line was one vast mass of torpedoes. The flower of the Cholacacan army were behind the walls, armed with the latest invented rifles, and altogether a siege of the capital would have lasted months. Don Hypolito, however, was too crafty to waste his time so fruitlessly, and artfully attacked the Republic in her weakest part.

Janjalla was but ill defended by walls and cannon

and but ill garrisoned with capable men. By throwing on the devoted town an overwhelming mass of troops he could hope to capture it within a few days. Then making it his head-quarters, could gradually advance along the plain towards the capital, eating up a town at every twenty miles. He was already master of Acauhtzin in the north, and if he could only reduce Janjalla and the four inland towns, he would be in complete command of the whole inner country. Then, besieging Tlatonac by land and sea, he could starve the capital into surrender.

Promptness was Xuarez' great characteristic, and so rapidly had he accomplished the transference of active operations from north to south that he had completely taken the Junta by surprise. It was a fatal mistake on the part of the Governmental party in leaving such an incapable man as Gomez at the head of affairs. If, relying on the strength of the capital to protect herself, he had sent all his available soldiers to garrison Janjalla and defeat the rebels before they could get a footing in the south, he would have probably crushed the rebellion in the bud. Victorious in the lower part of the country, he could

have then reduced Acauhtzin at his leisure, and thus
ended the war within a few weeks.

Unfortunately, Gomez lost his head at the critical
period, and proved himself quite unable to cope with
the masterly activity of the rebel leader.   First of all,
he committed the mistake of not concentrating his
troops at Janjalla, and then sent a few hundreds of
men down at a time. General Gigedo therefore found
himself shut up in Janjalla with scarcely a thousand
troops, few guns, and insufficient ammunition. The
telegraph-wires having been cut, he was unable to
communicate promptly with the capital, and being
in urgent need of reinforcements, was in absolute
despair as to what would occur in the near future. It
was true that Gomez had promised another thousand
men in ten days ; but, even if they arrived earlier, it
would be too late, as with the small garrison at his
disposal, it was impossible that he could hold out
against a force of six thousand for any lengthened
period.

He would have sent messengers to Tlatonac for aid,
but the troops of Don Hypolito completely encircled
the city, and it was worse than useless to try and

break through that girdle of steel. He held a council of war, but no decision could be arrived at, save that Janjalla should hold out, if possible, until reinforcements arrived from the capital. Day after day Gigedo and his staff swept the ocean with their glasses, looking for the torpederas and the cruiser. None of them appeared, and it could only be conjectured that they had captured *The Columbus*, and taken her at once to Tlatonac, in the harbour of which they were now doubtless lying.

Meanwhile, the garrison fought with desperate valour, and with great difficulty managed to keep the rebels at bay, but it could be easily seen that such a state of things could not last. On the fourth day preparations were made by Xuarez for a final assault, and everyone instinctively guessed that the end had come. *The Cortes* was lying with the transports out of range of the fort-guns, and, by means of their glasses, those shut up in the town could see that the warship was making ready to bombard the city.

Don Hypolito had come south again, with his new troops, and could be now seen riding about the camp with a brilliant staff, seeing that all things were ready for the assault. Jack, who, in company with Philip, was leaning over the ramparts, noted the audacious rebel, and remarked on his presence before the walls of Janjalla.

"There goes the brain of the rebellion," he said touching Philip on the shoulder. "If he could only be disposed of, the war would be over."

"No doubt. But Xuarez knows his own value too well, and will therefore keep out of danger. He has evidently made up his mind to finish the siege to-day."

"Unless help comes, I think he will succeed," replied Jack, gloomily. "I cannot conceive what the President or Maraquando can be thinking about to thus neglect Janjalla. If this town falls into the hands of Xuarez, as it must do, unless a miracle takes place, Don Francisco will find the war longer than he expects."

"Gomez is a fool," said Philip, stamping his foot. "What the deuce is the use of keeping all the army in the capital? There must be ten thousand soldiers shut up in Tlatonac, and his Excellency evidently intends to keep them there till Xuarez and his victorious troops arrive before the walls."

" Very likely the Indians are before the walls now, and are waiting for Xuarez to join them."

" It's not improbable. Things don't look promising for the Junta, and all because they let Gomez muddle the business. See, the rebels are marching up to the sea-gate. It is now noon. Before sundown they will be within the walls, and masters of the city."

" What about the garrison ? "

" Their lives depend on the caprice of Xuarez," said Philip, after a pause. " He may let Gigedo march out with the remains of his troop, or massacre every one of us."

" I don't intend to be massacred," replied Jack, dryly; " and, what is more, I don't intend to be seen by Xuarez. He must know by this time, through his spies, that I escaped from Totatzine, but he is probably ignorant that I am in Janjalla. I must escape unseen, Philip, else he will send me back to be slaughtered by Ixtlilxochitli."

" Hardly, Jack, while Tim is at hand ! "

" What do you mean ? "

" Don Hypolito," said Philip, sagely, " wishes to

stand well with the world. Tim is the medium through which his actions are reported to the world. Were he to send an Englishman to be offered up by savages to a barbaric deity, there would be trouble with England. Xuarez can't afford to risk that, so he will let you go free."

" He didn't do that in Acauhtzin."

" In Acauhtzin, my friend, you were supposed by us to be killed in the riot. He could do as he pleased with one, who, to the world was practically a non-existing person. Here it is different. You are alive, you are with your friends, one of whom is a correspondent of a great English journal. He dare not seize you for his own ends in broad daylight. No, my dear Jack, while we are beside you, Xuarez will think twice before repeating his treachery of Acauhtzin. He will have to look for a new victim for Ixtlilxochitli."

" I fervently hope and trust so," answered Jack, looking at his revolver to see that it was loaded. " And now I suppose we had better go to the Plaza. The troops must be assembling just now. Hark! there goes the trumpet. Where is Tim ?"

" In the telegraph-office, with Peter, wiring news to his paper."

" Poor Peter," said Duval, as they left the ramparts; "he came here to collect beetles, and finds himself plunged into an unpleasant war."

" Never mind.   There's nothing like experience, Jack.   Peter will recount his deeds of valour, even unto the third generation.   We will come out safe in the end.   You will marry Dolores, I Eulalia, and all will be gas and gaiters, *videlicet* Nicholas Nickleby."

Philip's gaiety was infectious, and Jack burst out laughing at his last remark.   They had no time, however, for further conversation, as the trumpets were calling loudly in the Plaza, and they hurried to that portion of the town to find the troops rapidly falling in.   General Gigedo made a speech to encourage his soldiers, assuring them that he had communicated with Tlatonac, and that relief would shortly come to the besieged town.

" Is that true, or a lie?" asked Jack of Don Sebastian, who stood beside him.

" True," replied the Spaniard, smiling.   " This morning carrier pigeons were sent to his Excellency

with messages of our deplorable state. We shall
certainly be relieved in a few days."

" A few days ! " echoed Philip, with a sneer. " My
dear Señor de Ahumada, a few hours will see our
troops evacuating Janjalla."

" If we are forced to do that, Señor, we can fall
back on Centeotl."

" What, with a few hundred men, and the Indians
scouring the country ? "

" They are further north."

" I assure you they are not," replied Cassim, emphatically. " We were attacked near Centeotl, and
by this time the savages are between that town and
this. Señor de Ahumada, I assure you that if we
evacuate Janjalla, we shall fall into the hands of the
Indians."

" Dios ! " cried Don Sebastian, suddenly. " *The
Cortes* has started bombarding." Even as he spoke
a bomb burst in the air directly over the Plaza. At
once Gigedo gave the signal to the troops to march
to the ramparts. In the distance they could hear the
fierce cries of the rebels as they marched out of
camp, and a tremour passed through the whole of the

city as those within its walls recognised the desperate
state of affairs.   Bomb after bomb exploded with
deafening noises, the troops manned the walls, the
besiegers hurled themselves against the sea-gate
and planted ladders against the walls.   The assault
had commenced.   It was the beginning of the end.

The full force at the disposal of General Gigedo,
excluding the sick and wounded, amounted to some
nine hundred men.   He divided this into two portions
five hundred held the sea-facing portion of the town
four hundred were stationed at the inland gate.
Xuarez attacked the two gates of the town simultaneously, and trusted, in the event of entering at
either portal, to be enabled to attack the loyalists
in the rear, and thus crush them between two
armies.

On the ramparts it was not so difficult to keep the
foe back as it was below.   They planted ladders, and
these were hurled with their burden of climbing men
into the ditch below.   An incessant fusillade of musketry crackled along the walls, and the cannon with
depressed muzzles hurled their balls with more or less
damaging effect into the dense throng massed on the

beach below. The bombs from *The Cortes* did their deadly work skilfully, and the besiegers kept themselves as widely apart as possible, so as to neutralise the effect of the shells on compact masses.

It was outside the sea-gate, however, that the siege was pressed most hardly. Xuarez had cannon planted at the gate, to break down, if possible, the huge wooden valves, clamped with iron. Through the loopholes low down in the walls the besiegers fired incessantly, killing the rebel gunners as they strove to discharge the cannon. Above the city hung a thick cloud of grey smoke, and at intervals, through the misty veil, flared the red flame of a bomb bursting overhead. The rattle of musketry, the booming of cannon, the cries of the wounded, the shouts of besieged and besiegers, all made an infernal din deafening to the ear.

Tim and Peter were at the land-gate in company with Captain Velez and Colonel Garibay, while Jack and Philip fought side by side in repelling the attack from the sea front. After an incessant cannonading lasting two hours, the rebels managed to smash the gates down with their artillery, and rushed in only to

find themselves confronted by a dense mass of resolute soldiery.

From the sea-gate the street arose suddenly, and
on the top of the incline Gigedo had planted cannon
which cut lanes in the throng of rebels pressing through
the gate. At last the battle resolved itself into a hand-
to-hand fight in which the loyalists strove to beat
back the rebel forces from the gate. Xuarez saw this,
and signalled to *The Cortes* to stand in closer and drop
her shells into the centre of the besieged. At once
the warship did as she was commanded, and in a few
moments bombs were creating fearful havoc in the
ranks of the loyalists. In answer, the guns of the forts
speedily opened fire on the warship, but did little
damage, as the besiegers were too busily occupied in
repelling the foe as they swarmed up the walls, to
take careful aim.

What with the dense crowd pressing from without,
the loss of men caused by the incessant bursting of
the bombs in their midst, the loyalists began to fall
back, and, in spite of the most desperate resistance,
were thrust beyond the line of cannon at the top of
the street. A horde of rebel soldiery rushed inside

the gate, and proceeded to scale the ramparts in order
to aid their comrades who were climbing the outer
walls, and to silence the guns playing on *The Cortes.*

Skilfully making use of all material he found to
hand, Xuarez turned the cannon taken from the loyalists on themselves. In the hurried retreat, they had
been unable to spike the guns, and now these, loaded
and fired by the rebels, were mowing them down in
dozens. The soldiers on the ramparts were either
killed or beaten back, and the whole of the sea front
of Janjalla was in complete possession of Xuarez.
One comfort had the loyalists, namely, that they
were protected in the rear by their men defending
the land-gate.

Shortly, however, a roar of rage, and the cheers of
the besiegers announced that the town was captured
on that side. The soldiers retreated towards the
Plaza in the centre of the town, and there found their
comrades who had fallen back from the sea-gate.
Here there was this handful of men shut up in the
square, surrounded on all sides by the victorious
rebels. They could not possibly hold out long
against the dense masses converging to that centre

from all parts of the town, and it could be easily seen
that the siege was practically over.

During the fighting night had fallen, and now the
battle was going on in the dim twilight, rendered still
darker by the heavily hanging clouds of smoke en-
wrapping the town. Jack had received a nasty cut on
the shoulder ; but Philip was unwounded, and in the
general scrimmage they managed to keep well
together. When beaten back into the Plaza, they
made for the telegraph-office, where they hoped to
find Tim and Peter. This was the rendezvous ap-
pointed by Tim in case the battle went in favour of
the rebels, as he wished to send a final message to his
paper before clearing out of the town. With a handful of men, principally those belonging to their own
regiment, Philip and Jack managed to throw themselves into the telegraph-office, and shortly afterwards were joined by Tim.

"Where's Peter?" asked Jack, as he saw the huge
form of his friend dashing through the door.

"Just behind, with Don Sebastian," gasped Tim,
throwing himself into a chair. "It's all up, boys; the
Opposidores are in full possession of the land-gate."

"And the sea-gate also," said Philip, who was re-loading his revolver. "All our men are in the Plaza, and can't hold out much longer. Whew! there's another bomb."

"We'd better get out of Janjalla, and make for Centeotl," cried Don Sebastian, entering with his sword smashed in two; "all is over!"

"Gigedo?"

"Killed! Garibay is wounded, and taken prisoner!"

"Where is Don Pedro?"

"Here I am," cried Peter, darting into the room and closing the door. "There's a regiment of rebels cutting their way through the crowd to take the tele-graph-office. Xuarez has particularly commanded it."

"Anyhow, I'll have time to send another telegram, if I die for it," said Tim, who was hastily scribbling notes. "Where's Manuel?"

Manuel had vanished; so Tim, with a growl, sat down to work the instrument himself.

"Keep those devils out, with your men," he said to Philip, who was barricading the windows with Jack. "I'll send one telegram, saying Janjalla has fallen, and then we'll go off."

" How the devil are we to get away ? " asked Philip, angrily.

" Easily.   The cavalry barracks are behind here. We'll get round by the back way and seize the horses, then cut our way out by the land-gate.   Once across the river, and we are safe."

Philip did not wait for the conclusion of this speech, but, with a few men, dashed out at the back of the house to see if the horses were still there.   Jack would have followed, but Peter stopped him.

" I have my medicine-chest here.   Let me bind up your shoulder."   Jack was unwilling, protesting he did not feel the wound.

" Bosh, my dear boy, you are excited.   You will feel it afterwards.   If we are to ride to Centeotl, you will need all the blood you have.   Don Sebastian can hold the telegraph-office."

Don Sebastian had posted his men at the windows, and was firing at the mass of rebels, now trying to take the house by storm.   All this time Tim was working the instrument and wiring the news of the fall of the city to his editor.   Through the yells outside, the rattle of the musketry, and the curses of

Don Sebastian could be heard the incessant click, click, click of the telegraph-instrument.

A bomb exploded on the roof of the house, and a few yards of plaster fell from the ceiling. Peter had finished binding up Jack's wound, and now they were both defending the windows and doors of the mansion.

" How long, Jack ? "

" In two minutes the door will be down," cried Jack. " Do leave that d——d instrument, Tim, and look for Philip."

" I'll go ! " said Peter, as Tim refused to leave his post. He turned to make for the back way, when Philip came back with a radiant face.

" Here is a dozen horses just outside, all saddled and fresh as daisies ! Come, Tim, quick ! Jack. De Ahumada."

" A moment," said Tim, and went on with his clicking.

Crash ! The door was down, and a number of fierce faces appeared at the door. The room was full of smoke, and the rebels were firing freely through the windows. Sebastian and his men threw them-

selves in front of those trying to face the door, and ·
Philip, seizing Tim by the shoulder, dragged him away
from the instrument.

"Tim, you cursed fool. Come along!"

"Just a second!"

He turned back to the instrument in spite of
Philip's protest, but had just clicked twice when Don
Sebastian and his men were forced back and a crowd
of the enemy rushed into the room. Philip, Jack, and
Peter had already disappeared through the back, and
Tim was left alone with Don Sebastian and the
soldiers. The rebels threw themselves forward with
yells of delight, when Tim, catching up a heavy table,
flung it fair on the advancing mass, then bolted
through the back door, dragging Don Sebastian after
him. Two of the soldiers followed, and promptly
closed the door when on the right side. At once the
rebels commenced to beat it down with the butts of
their rifles, but the Irishman and his friend had
reached the back street.

Here they found their friends already mounted and
waiting for them.

"Tim. De Ahumada! Mount at once!" cried

Philip, pointing to three horses waiting under the shelter of the wall. "Make for the land-gate, and straight for the river."

In another moment they were clattering towards the lower part of the town, keeping close together for safety. The street down which they were riding was quite deserted, as the fighting was principally confined to the main thoroughfares of the town. They could hear the brisk fire of musketry still kept up, the booming of the cannon, and the bursting of the shells. Shrieks of women, and yells of the victors broke incessantly through these noises, and the whole city was draped in a thick veil of stinking smoke.

"Oh, those poor women!" cried Philip, as he spurred his horse towards the gate. "Now they are in the clutches of those fiends."

"I'm glad we're not," muttered Dr. Grench, thankfully.

"Anyhow," said Tim, cheerfully, "I've sent the fall of the city to the paper."

"Oh, hang your paper," said Jack, whose wound was making him fractious. "Come along, De Ahumada."

"Dios! How we have been beaten."

Suddenly the street turned a sharp angle, and they found themselves before the gate. Most of the attacking party had marched towards the centre of the town to complete their victory, and only a few scattered soldiery were on guard. These yelled loudly as they saw the small party dash towards the gate. The valves were broken down; beyond was the country, and between this and safety was but a score of men.

Philip drew his sword, spurred his horse to its full speed, and made for the gate, cutting down a man who tried to stay him. Jack emptied two barrels of his revolver, and killed one man, wounding another. The rebel soldiers fired freely, and breaking Sebastian's arm, also tumbled one of his company off his horse. Tim seizing Peter's bridle-rein, galloped wildly through the spare crowd, cursing freely.

In their rush for the portal, they scattered them all. There were a few musket-shots, a howl of rage from the disappointed rebels, and at top speed they tore out of the gate, and made for the open country.

"Twenty miles," cried Philip, settling himself in his saddle. "We can do that easily. Hurrah!"

" Provided we don't fall into the hands of the Indians," said Jack, sagely.

As for Don Sebastian, he turned round and shook his fist at Janjalla.

" Carajo ! "

CHAPTER III.

THE FLIGHT TO TLATONAC.

Boot and saddle, away! away!
We must be far e'er the breaking of day.
   The standard is down,
   The foe's in the town,
Forbidding us longer to stay, to stay.

Boot and saddle! we ride! we ride!
Over the prairie land side by side,
   Our foemen behind,
   Speed swift as the wind,
And gain on us steadily, stride by stride.

Boot and saddle! so fast! so fast!
We ride till the river be crossed and past ;
   Then over the plain,
   With loose-hanging rein,
And find ourselves safe in the town at last.

BEFORE them spread the plains, flat and desolate-looking, covered with coarse grass, and stretching towards the horizon in vague immensity. Westward the faint flush of sunset, delicately pale, lingered low down, but otherwise the sky was coldly clear, darkly blue, thick sprinkled with chill-looking stars. To the right the leaden-hued waters of the river moving sluggishly between low mud banks, and on the left sandy wastes, alternating with hillocks and convex-shaped mounds. All this desolation appearing ghostly under a veil of mist exhaled whitely from the hot earth.

Over these monotonous plains galloped the six fugitives. Philip and Jack in the van, Don Sebastian and his one soldier in the rear; between Tim, side by side with Peter. For some time they urged on their horses in silence. Then a sudden flare of crimson caused them to turn in their saddles. The low walls of Janjalla were crowned with smoke, beneath which leaped tongues of flame, crimson and yellow. A rapid, disjointed conversation ensued.

" Those brutes are burning the city ! "

" It will only be some drunken soldiers. Xuarez will soon put a stop to that. He cannot afford to lose his city of refuge, after paying so much to gain it."

" Must we swim our horses across the river? " called out Grench, unexpectedly.

" Not unless the bridge is down. It was standing when we came this way a week ago."

Philip answered the question, and then cast an anxious look at the sky.

"I wish the moon would rise," he said disconsolately; "we need some light."

"What the deuce would be the good of that when we're on the high-road. Hang it, the moon would only show Xuarez how to follow us."

"Que dici?" asked Don Sebastian, looking at Jack.

"The Señor Corresponsal thinks we might be pursued."

"I doubt it, Don Juan. Xuarez will be too busy checking the excesses of his soldiers. Besides, Señor, as we escaped in the confusion, it may be that we will not be missed for some hours."

Peter, unaccustomed to riding, began to feel sore with this incessant galloping, and raised his voice in protest.

"I hope we will be able to rest at Centeotl. When do we reach it?"

"Before midnight, probably. Then we will rest till dawn, get fresh horses, and push on to Tlatonac."

"Hope we'll get there," muttered Jack, shaking his reins. "But if the Indians——"

"Deuce take the Indians," retorted Philip, irrit-
ably. "Come on Jack, and don't worry so much."

Their horses were fortunately quite fresh, having
been mewed up in Janjalla without exercise for
some weeks. Stretching their necks, they clattered
along at a breakneck speed. The road was as hard
as flint, and their iron-shod hoofs struck out sparks
from the loose stones. The riders, with their heads
bent against the wind whizzing past their ears, let
the reins hang loosely, and pressed on with blind
trust along the highway leading to Centeotl.

Here and there they passed a flat-roofed house,
deserted by its occupants, and standing up lonely,
a white splotch amid the vague gloom of its flat acre-
age. Clumps of trees loomed suddenly against the
clear sky, at times a ragged aloe sprang spectral-like
from the reddish soil, thorny thickets lay densely in
the hollows, tall spear-grass waved on the tops of un-
dulating drifts of sand, and at intervals an oasis of
rank herbage would frame an oval pool thickly
fringed with reeds.

The road wound onward, turning now to right, now
to left, dipping into hollows, curving over eminences,

stretching white and dusty towards the horizon like a crooked winding river. On either side they could mark the moving forms of animals, flying from the clatter of their horses' hoofs, cattle, vicuñas, llamas, and flocks of sheep. The white peak of Xicotencatl arose suddenly like a ghost from the shadows of forests lying heavily along the verge of earth between plain and sky. A thin vapour lay white over the plain, and gathered thickly along the banks of the river. The horses stretched their necks and neighed loudly. They smelt the water of the stream.

" The bridge is down !" cried Jack, drawing rein at the verge of the stream. " Indians !"

" Or Xuarez !" added Philip, gravely. " I suspect the latter. Indians are not sufficiently civilised to destroy bridges."

The _débris_ of the bridge impeded the current, and here the waters boiled white amid the black ruins. Jagged posts stretched in black rows to the other side of the stream, but there was no foothold left by which they could cross dry-shod.

"Swim !" said Tim, briefly, and sent his steed down the bank. The others followed, and in a few

minutes the surface of the stream was dotted with
black figures. The river being sluggish, with little or
no current, they found no difficulty in crossing, and
speedily gained the opposite bank. Climbing the
slope on to the flat land, they regained the line of
road, and once more urged their horses to full speed.

The moon arose, round and bright, making the
whole scene cheerful with her kindly light. The
fugitives looked back, but could see no sign of pursuit.
Even the town had vanished. Behind, before, lay
nothing but the immensity of the plains. It was as
though they were in the midst of a leaden-hued sea.
The appearance of the moon raised their spirits, and
they redoubled their speed. Centeotl was now
comparatively near. The ground began to show
signs of cultivation. Hedges of cacti ran along the
sides of the road, bearing fleshly looking flowers of
tawny gold. Right and left stretched gardens, en-
vironing country houses, and before them arose a
white line of wall.

" Centeotl !" cried Don Sebastian, pushing forward.

The gates were closed owing to the fear of the
townspeople lest the Indians should make a night

attack. De Ahumada galloped on ahead, and reined
his horse immediately under the walls. At intervals
the sentinels called the one to the other, " Centinella
alerte," to show that they were awake. The noise of
the approaching horses brought them to the walls.

" Quien vive ! "

"Amigos ! From Janjalla."

The red light of torches glared from the low battlements, and in a few minutes the gates were opened.
The officer in charge recognised Don Sebastian, and
was much depressed at learning Janjalla had fallen.

" Dios ! It is Centeotl next that Xuarez will capture," he said, disconsolately, and then led the fugitives to the house of the Jefe Politico.

That individual received them kindly, and gave them
food and beds. He also promised them horses for the
next morning, to push on to Tlatonac, but feared lest
they should fall into the hands of the Indians, whom
he believed were further north. The telegraph-wires
between Centeotl and Hermanita had been destroyed
by the savages. His town was now quite isolated in
the plains. Only five hundred men were within its
walls, and he expected it would be shortly besieged

and captured by Don Hypolito, unless aid arrived from the capital.

During the night straggling parties of soldiers arrived from Janjalla for refuge. All brought the same tale. Janjalla was nearly in ruins, as the rebels had fired many houses, and the bombs and cannon had smashed others. Xuarez had kept all his men in the town, and was doing his best to reduce them to order; but many were beyond his control. There was no pursuit in any case. It was reported that he would throw forward two regiments of cavalry next day, to attack Centeotl.

"Santissima!" said the Jefe, in despair; "we are lost, Señores. When you arrive at Tlatonac, tell his Excellency that I am faithful to the Junta, but that my town is too weak to hold out against the rebels."

De Ahumada promised and shortly afterwards, thoroughly worn out, they all composed themselves to sleep. It was impossible, however, to get much repose, as the constant arrival of fugitives, the clattering of horses through the streets, and the murmur of many voices, kept them awake. At dawn they were up at once, mounted fresh horses, and rode away

E 2

from the town in the direction of Hermanita, twenty miles away.

They reached that town in two hours, and found the inhabitants in a state of terror. The Indians had been threatening for the last week, and had been scouring the country to the south. Now they had gone north, and, it was believed, with the intention of making an attack on the Puebla de los Naranjos. Nor did the news brought by Jack and his friends reassure them in any way. What with the Indians in the north, and Xuarez threatening them in the south, there was no doubt that Hermanita was in a terrible fix. As had Centeotl, they also implored Don Sebastian to ask Gomez to send aid, lest they should fall victims to the rebels or to the Indians.

After taking a hurried meal, the fugitives once more proceeded on their way to the north. Towards noon they struck Puebla de los Naranjos, and found it a heap of ruins. Undefended as were the other towns by stone walls, the town was surrounded by orange groves, and had therefore been easily captured by the Indians. A few terrified survivors crept about the ruins of their houses, the streets were thick with dead bodies, and the whole place presented a scene of unexampled desolation. Those folks who survived said that the Indians had plundered the town two days previously, and had then departed with the intention of taking Chichimec. As this city was only distant twenty miles from the capital, the little party was quite appalled at the audacity of the savages. It showed how little they cared for the power of the Republic.

"If Gomez had crushed this rebellion at once, all would have been well," said Jack, as they rode from the smoking ruins of Puebla de los Naranjos; "but now it seems as though the Indians and Xuarez were going to have it all their own way."

"Gomez should have placed the command of affairs in the hands of a competent man, and not meddled with them," replied Philip, impatiently. "He keeps all his army in the capital, and lets the country be laid waste. The end will be that all the inland towns will join with Xuarez, and the capital will be besieged. With the whole of Cholacaca against it, the capital must fall."

"Unless the Junta can capture or sink the two

remaining warships of Xuarez," said Don Sebastian, who was fearfully enraged at the destruction of the country.

"True! Then Xuarez won't be able to get more troops from Acauhtzin."

"He has got quite enough troops, as it is to make things unpleasant for the capital," said Tim, in Spanish, for the benefit of Don Sebastian. "Six thousand at Janjalla—five thousand Indians. Quite enough to invest the town. The Junta has but eight thousand troops in Tlatonac."

"Well, that's a good number!"

"Yes; but what with his own troops and the savages, Xuarez has three thousand to the good. Besides which, he is a capable general."

"If the Indians could only be detached from his cause, the rebellion might be crushed," said Jack, ponderingly. "It is the only way of saving the present Government."

"There is no chance of doing that," replied Tim, disconsolately. "The Indians are mad about the loss of the opal, and will fight like fiends to get it back."

" Perhaps they can be quietened by means of the opal ! "

" Dios ! " exclaimed Sebastian, turning in his saddle. " What mean you, Señor ? "

" I have an idea," replied Jack, quietly. " It was suggested to me by a remark of Cocom's."

" And this idea ? "

" I will not tell you at present, lest I should fail to carry it out, and thus disappoint your hopes. Wait till we reach Tlatonac."

" If we ever do get there," muttered Philip, savagely. " Now we are half way to Chichimec, gentlemen. There, according to report, the Indians are camped. I vote we make a detour, and reach Tlatonac in some other way. Do you know of a road, Don Sebastian?"

" No, Señor. I know not this country."

" I do ! " cried Duval, suddenly. " I have been all over this portion. That is a good idea of yours, Philip ! We must avoid the Indians. I know a road ! "

" Bueno ! Take the lead."

It was fortunate, indeed, that Philip suggested such an idea, and that Jack's knowledge of the country

enabled them to carry it out, else they would
assuredly have fallen into the hands of the Indians.
Making a detour towards the coast, they managed to
avoid Chichimec by some miles.   They learned from
a peon, whom they met making his way to Tlatonac,
that the town was entirely invested by the savages,
but that as yet, thanks to the strong walls, they had
been unable to effect an entrance.   The Jefe Politico
had sent this peon to the capital with a request for
immediate aid from Don Francisco.

"What, in God's name, can the President be thinking about?" cried Jack, on hearing this intelligence.
"He is simply playing into the hands of his enemies."

"Things certainly look bad for the Junta, owing
to his negligence.   Janjalla captured by Xuarez.
Puebla de los Naranjos ravaged, Chichimec invested.
Perhaps, when the whole country is in the hands of
Don Hypolito, this very wise ruler will bestir him-
self."

"Wait till I have a conversation with Don Miguel!"
muttered Jack, striking the spurs into his horse. "We
are outsiders, and cannot interfere with local politics;
but it makes me sick to see how Gomez is fooling

away his chances. If I can only rouse Don Miguel into making things hot for the President, I shall do so!"

" A house divided against itself—— " began Peter ; but Tim cut him short.

" Hold your tongue, Peter. Jack is quite right. Unless a good man is put at the head of affairs, Don Hypolito will enter Tlatonac within the month. It's a mighty black look-out for the Government. Don Francisco ought to be shunted at once."

The peon ran alongside them, and kept up with their horses in the most wonderful manner. It was noon when they left Puebla de los Naranjos, and it was now late at night. In ten hours they had come nearly fifty miles. Their horses were quite worn out, owing to the incessant galloping. Now they were within a mile of the capital, and already, in the dim light, could see the line of walls looming in the distance. They were glad it was dark, or, rather, comparatively so, as it afforded them a certain amount of protection from wandering Indian scouts.

" The luck holds ! " said Philip, thankfully, as they rode towards the Puerta de la Culebra. " We have not seen a single savage since we left Janjalla."

" Had it not been for your forethought, Philip, they would have had our scalps by this time."

" My thought, but your actions, Jack. It was lucky you knew the country."

"A mutual admiration society, you are!" cried Tim, whose spirits were wonderfully light. " How do you feel, Peter ? "

"Worn out," replied the doctor, laconically.

"Faith. I'm not astonished. I'm bumped to death also. A hundred miles isn't bad for an inferior rider like myself."

"Oh, you are a war correspondent," began Peter, fretfully, when his remarks were cut short by an ex- clamation from Sebastian.

"Dios! the gates are open! Soldiers are coming out!"

" Reinforcements for Janjalla. I've no doubt," said Philip, grimly. " They are a trifle late. Come, gentle- men, let us see the officer in charge."

They urged their jaded horses towards the gate. At the sight of the little party, the soldiers halted, and an officer rode to the front.

" From whence come you, Señores ? " he asked in surprise.

" From Janjalla."

" Janjalla ?   Why, we are just marching thither, Señor."

" You can spare yourself the trouble ! " replied Jack, grimly.   " Janjalla has fallen."

The news passed rapidly from mouth to mouth, and a cry of rage went up from the throng.

" Moreover," added Jack, quietly.   " Puebla de los Naranjos has been attacked and sacked by the Indians ! "

Another cry of rage.

"And," concluded this bearer of bad news," Chichimec is now invested by six thousand savages."

A low murmur of dismay ran through the lines. Calamity after calamity seemed to be falling on the heads of the Government. Suddenly a man rode through the gate at full speed, and pulling up his horse on its haunches, as he faced the party, made the same inquiry as had the officer.

" Janjalla," cried Don Miguel Maraquando.

Jack uttered the same reply.

" Janjalla has fallen ! "

CHAPTER IV.

EXIT DON FRANCISCO GOMEZ.

Depart, incapable !
You are no pilot to be at the helm when the ship is in danger ;
The vessel of state labours in the turmoil of troublous waters,
Rocks this side, that side, she is drifting to leeward, shoals threaten
    her stout timbers.
Round her rage the tempests which would sink her in waves of blood ;
Only a skilful captain can pilot her into a safe haven.
You are not a skilful commander !
In fair weather you guided the ship in a meritorious fashion ;
Now, when blow rebellious storms, you are not fit for the steering ;
    the danger renders you helpless—a child were a better helmsman ;
No longer can you hold the ship of Republican fortunes in her right
    course.
Captain ! President ! you are Captain—President no longer !
Depart ! give way to one who can steer with clear head and keen eye.
Depart, incapable !

" DEAR one ! " cried Dolores, as Jack embraced her, in the patio. "At last do I see you once more. Santissima ! how pale ! What ragged clothes ! and beards on all your faces."

" Indeed, Dolores, a siege is not conducive to luxury.

But we will go to my house ; bath, shave, and dress. When we return, you will behold us as civilised beings."

" You are wounded ! "

" It is nothing—a mere scratch. How delighted I am to see your dear face once more, my Dolores."

Eulalia put out her hand timidly under the shelter of her fan, and touched Philip gently on the hand. She was unable to do more, as Doña Serafina, severe, and vigilant, was present. Their engagement had not yet been made public.

" Querido," she murmured, looking at her lover tenderly. " Constantly have I prayed for thee."

Philip kissed her hand, and then that of Doña Serafina, to avert suspicion. The old lady was voluble, and after the first greetings were over, burst forth into speech with much dramatic gesture.

" Alas, señores ! How sad look you all. Don Pedro ! Pobrecito ! And the city is in the hands of the rebels. Ay di mi ! Ah, the evil ones ! Yet, if they win on land, they lose at sea."

" What is it you say, Señora ? " asked Tim, ever on the alert for news.

"Have you not heard, Señor Corresponsal?"
No; you have been away. Gracios á Dios! The
torpederas have captured *The Columbus*."

"Bravo!" cried Jack, delightedly; "this is indeed
good news! And Rafael?"

"Rafael is here," said that young man, hastily entering the court. "Ah, my dear friends, how delighted
I am to behold you."

"Even though we bring bad news?"

"Yes; for I can tell you good. We followed
The Columbus, and by threatening to sink her with
torpedoes, forced her to strike her flag. Now she is
lying in the harbour, with a crew of our own men.
Her rebel sailors are all in prison."

"What about *The Iturbide?*"

"She is there also, but in a crippled condition.
One of her masts was shot away by *The Columbus*
before she surrendered."

"And what do you do now?"

"Sail south to-morrow at dawn."

"Alas!" said Jack, sadly, "you will be too late to
relieve Janjalla."

"Never mind," replied Rafael, hopefully; "we

shall capture or sink *The Cortes*, and bring her back to Tlatonac with the transports. Then Don Hypolito will be irrevocably cut off from Acauhtzin."

"That does not matter to him," interposed Philip, overhearing this remark; "he has most of his troops at Janjalla, and will simply hold the south instead of the north."

"At all events, Señor Felipe, we have crushed him by sea."

"It will be a more difficult task to crush him by land, especially as Don Francisco is so dilatory."

"Don Francisco! Don Francisco!" cried Rafael, stamping his foot with rage. "He is not fit to be President. Through him have we lost Janjalla. Even my father, who was his firm supporter, has turned against him."

"What do you say, Rafael?"

"I cannot tell you yet; but there will be a stormy meeting of the Junta to-morrow."

"You are going to depose Don Francisco."

"It's not improbable."

"More trouble," said Tim, reflectively. "There

will be three Presidents shortly. Don Francisco, Don Hypolito, and—Don Miguel!"

"No more, mi amigo," said Rafael, doubtful even in his own house. "It is dangerous to speak like that—as yet."

He added the last words significantly, and turned away. Jack was saying good night to Dolores, as he was quite worn out, and wanted to get back to his own house for a good night's rest.

"Dolores," he whispered, as he held her hand; "you have yet the opal?"

"Yes; surely."

"Can you bear to part with it for the sake of the city?"

"You can do with it as you please, Juanito. But, what mean these words?"

"I have a plan whereby I can detach the Indians from the cause of Don Hypolito, and thus weaken his army. But the carrying out of the plan may entail the loss of the opal."

"Let it go, so that it save Tlatonac," replied Dolores, heroically, though, woman-like, she loved the jewel. "What is your plan?"

" I must see Cocom about it first. Then I will
tell you my secret; but now we must go. Adios,
querida."

When the four friends left the Casa Maraquando,
they were surprised to find themselves followed by
Maraquando and his son. On reaching Jack's house,
Don Miguel begged the Englishman to give him a
few moments' conversation, and explained how matters
stood at Tlatonac.

It appeared that Maraquando's party were dis-
gusted at the way in which the war was being conducted by Don Francisco, and wanted him to resign
the Presidential chair. This Gomez was unwilling
to do, and as he had yet many supporters, it was
doubtful if they could force him into such a course.
Now, however, that the news of the fall of Janjalla,
the sack of Puebla de los Naranjos, and the invest-
ment of Chichimec had arrived, Don Miguel thought
that he would be able to show plainly that the con-
tinuance of Don Francisco as President meant ruin
to the Government.

The next day there was to be a meeting of the
Junta, and Maraquando, explaining his designs to

Jack, asked him for a full report of all that had taken place in the south, so as to plainly prove the incapacity of the President in conducting the war. The four friends thoroughly agreed with Maraquando's view of the matter, and told him all that he wished to know, after which they retired to rest. Don Miguel, on the contrary, went back with Rafael to his own house, and there found a few members of his party waiting him, whom he informed of the consequence of the terrible series of blunders made by Gomez.

The next day there was a stormy debate of the Junta in the Palacio Nacional.

"I blame his Excellency for all that has taken place," cried Maraquando, at the conclusion of a long and fiery speech. "By his negligence and timidity he has lost us our opportunity of crushing this rebellion in the bud. Had a few thousand soldiers been sent to Janjalla at the outbreak of the war, that city would not now be in the hands of the rebels. Nay, they would not have even gained a footing in the south. But, by withdrawing the garrisons from that seaport, from the inland towns, his Excellency had laid them open to capture, and they had been captured. Janjalla is in the power of Xuarez ; by this time, for aught we know, Centeotl may have surrendered to his victorious army. Puebla de los Naranjos has been sacked by the Indian tribes, who should have been crushed at once. Now Chichimec is surrounded, and may fall at any time, yet no aid has been sent to the relief of the citizens. All these terrible disasters have been caused by the blundering of Don Francisco, by his incompetency. I call on him to resign his command into more capable hands, else will we see the foe at our gates, our city in ruins, and Cholacaca helpless, under the heel of the tyrant Xuarez !"

Don Francisco, bursting with indignation, replied, He had done his best ! If he had sent forward troops to Janjalla, they might have been defeated, and then the capital would have fallen an easy prey to the rebels, through lack of garrison. As it was, the city could hold out for months ; the walls were strong, the garrison were resolute, there was plenty of provisions.

He had held the army at Tlatonac to save the capital. Where, then, was the blunder in that ? By sea, the forces of the Republic had been victorious. *The Pizarro* had been sunk, *The Columbus* captured, and now the torpederas were on their way to Janjalla harbour to force *The Cortes* to strike her flag. He had succeeded by sea. He would succeed on land. When the army of Xuarez was before the walls of Tlatonac the fate of the country could be decided in one battle. He refused to resign his position as President.

The partisans of Maraquando, the supporters of Gomez, broke out into noisy demonstrations, and the whole place was in an uproar. The one called upon Gomez to resign, the other denounced Maraquando as a traitor. It seemed as though neither would give in, as though the capital would be divided into two hostile factions, when a solution of the difficulty was proposed by Padre Ignatius.

Making his appearance suddenly in the hall, the good priest first stilled the tumult by holding up his crucifix, and then begged to lay before the Junta a proposition which would suit all parties. It would never do, said the Padre, to depose Don Francisco. The pretext for war, alleged by Xuarez, was that Gomez ought to be deposed for breaking the Constitution of Cholacaca. They knew that His Excellency had not done so; that he had loyally upheld the freedom and laws of the Republic. If deposed by his own party, such a deposition would give colour to Xuarez's assertion that he had right on his side, and perhaps prejudice the inland towns in his favour. Better it would be to let Don Francisco still remain President till the date of the expiration of his office, four months hence, and in the meantime entrust the conduct of the war solely to Don Miguel Maraquando. By this arrangement his Excellency would still continue nominal head of Cholacaca, and the war could be conducted by Maraquando, without the responsibility resting on the President.

This proposition, seeming to be the only possible solution of the problem, was unanimously accepted by both parties. It is true that Gomez, who hated Maraquando like poison, sorely grudged giving up the command of affairs to his rival; but as he saw that the Junta wished it to be so, he was forced to yield. Don Miguel was, therefore, elected General of the army of the Republic, and Don Francisco was permitted to retain the civil rule. Then the meeting broke up, and Maraquando went off to take measures for the immediate relief of Chichimec, while Gomez, much mortified at the slight he had received, retired sullenly to his palace. -

"What's the matter, Tim?" asked Jack, as they left the Palacio Nacional. "You ought to be pleased at witnessing such a stirring scene, instead of which you are like a bear with a sick head."

"And haven't I a cause?" replied Tim, gruffly. "Look at all this shindy going on, and I can't send a telegram to my paper."

"Oh, that's it, is it? Well, then, ask Philip to lend you *The Bohemian*, and go off to Truxillo at once."

"Begad, that isn't a bad idea anyhow," cried Tim, stopping suddenly; "but I don't want to leave Tlatonac just now."

"Well, you may be pretty certain Philip won't go, nor I. Why not send Peter? Write out your news here. Peter will take it, and old Benker will look after the yacht."

"How far is it to Truxillo?"

"A trifle over three hundred miles."

"Do you think Philip will lend me the yacht?"

"I'm sure he will. Let us ask him at once. He is flirting with Doña Eulalia in Maraquando's patio."

Tim, who had quite recovered his spirits at Jack's happy suggestion, started off at once to the Casa Maraquando. There was no necessity, however, for them to go so far, for they met their friend coming down the Calle Otumba. He hailed them at once.

"Tim! Jack! come along to the Puerta de la Culebra. News from Chichimec."

"What do you say?" roared Tim, plunging towards the speaker.

"Cocom came to the Casa Maraquando a few minutes ago, and told me that a messenger had arrived from Chichimec. He is at the Puerta de la Culebra."

"The deuce!" cried Jack, in alarm, as they hurried along towards the gate; "perhaps it's another request for relief."

"If so, they will soon have it," said Tim, quickly. "Don Miguel is going to send three thousand men this day to finish off these savages."

"Ah, that is something like!" said Philip, approvingly; "there will be some chance of relieving the city with that force. I am glad Don Miguel has matters now in his own hands."

"So am I. He'll end the war in no time. I say, Philip, lend me the yacht."

"What for? You are not going to Janjalla again?"

"No! I'm going further south. That is, I'm sending Peter with despatches."

"Where to?"

"Truxillo! He can send off my telegrams from there. Lend me the yacht, Philip, and I'll love you for ever more."

"Oh, take her, by all means; but I hope she won't be smashed up by the warships of Xuarez."

"He's only got one now," replied Tim, coolly; "and she'll have her hands full looking after the torpederas."

"I forgot that! It's a good idea, Tim! Get all the news together you can, and Peter shall go out with *The Bohemian* to-night, both of them in charge of Benker."

"Do you think Peter will go?" said Jack, doubt-fully.

"Of course he will," said Tim, promptly. "The little man's of no use here. I'll make him Queen's messenger for once in his life."

" Hallo!" cried Philip, at this moment, " there's old Cocom making signs. Ola, Cocom!"

The old Indian, who was hobbling on the other side of the street, came over to them with an excited look on his usually immobile face.

" Carambo, Señores! the news. The terrible news!"

" What is it?" cried the three Englishmen simultaneously.

" Chichimec has fallen!"

Jack uttered an ejaculation of rage, and darted off to the gate, followed by Tim and Philip. They found an excited throng of people talking wildly together. Don Sebastian was just under the archway, with his glasses to his eyes, looking towards the plains beyond.

" Is the news true of Chichimec's fall?" asked Jack pushing his way through the crowd.

Don Sebastian turned slowly with a grave bow, and handed Jack the glasses.

"Quite true, Señor. See! fugitives are arriving every moment."

Jack clapped the glass to his eye, and saw that the plain was sprinkled with people all making for the gate of Tlatonac.

"Why don't you send out a regiment to protect them, De Ahumada?"

"It is going now. Behold, Señor."

About five hundred men, well mounted, came trotting down the street, and began to file through the archway out on to the plain. Jack stood on one side and watched them go by in all their martial splendour.

"How did the Indians take the town, De Ahumada?"

"It was surprised last night," replied Don Sebastian, sadly. "I expect the sentinels were worn out with constant watching. Dios! It is frightful. First Puebla de los Naranjos, now Chichimec; Janjalla has already fallen, and Tlatonac——"

"Won't fall," interrupted Jack, abruptly, as the last of the cavalry swept through the gate. "When things are at their worst, matters mend. Just now they are very gloomy. To-morrow they may improve."

Tim stayed behind to make inquiries about the fall of Chichimec for the use of his paper, and Philip, in company with Jack, went off to look up Peter, and ask him if he would consent to act as Tim's messenger to Truxillo. They could not find him in their own house, and learned from a servant that he had gone in search of them to the Casa Maraquando. At once they repaired thither, and had just reached the door, when Peter, with a look of alarm on his face, rushed out of the house, almost falling into their arms in his hurry.

" Philip ! Jack ! Have you heard ? "

" What is the matter, Peter ? "

" Don Francisco has shot himself ! Don Miguel has just told me."

Philip made a gesture of horror, and Jack ran into the house to see Maraquando, and learn the particulars of the case.

It was perfectly true. Unable to bear the disgrace of being deposed from the active conduct of affairs, President Gomez had retired to his room, and shot himself through the heart.

CHAPTER V.

THE INDIAN RAID.

Painted braves came on the war-path,
Numerous as the leaves in summer,
Decked with feathers and with wampum,
All their faces fierce and fearless,
Streaked with colours like the sunset,
Rage was in their hearts of iron ;
Spears grasped they, and bows and arrows,
And their horses, like the storm clouds,
Swiftly swept across the prairies,
Till the firm earth shook and trembled
'Neath the thunder of their thousands.
Loud they sang the song of battle,
Sang the song of war and bloodshed ;
While the nations, women-hearted,
Hid within their wallèd cities,
Like the rabbits in their burrows,
When they heard that chaunt triumphal.

CERTAINLY, fate was dealing hardly with the Republic of Cholacaca. One blow followed another, and it seemed as though the final catastrophe would be the triumphal entry of Don Hypolito Xuarez into the capital. Janjalla was in his possession; he now threatened Centeotl, and the two towns of Puebla de los Naranjos and Chichimec had been destroyed by his savage allies. The unexpected death of Don Francisco Gomez put the finishing touch to this series of calamities, and the whole city was pervaded by a feeling of dismay. Disquieting rumours crept among the people that Xuarez had captured Centeotl and Hermanita—that he was now on his way to Tlatonac—that the death of President Gomez was due to his machinations. These fabrications, gaining additions as they flew from mouth to mouth, carried fear into the hearts of the citizens, and many were of the opinion that nothing was left save surrender to the insolent conqueror.

The Junta met within an hour of the intelligence of Don Francisco's death, and unanimously elected Don Miguel Maraquando as President of the Republic. Even the party of the dead ruler supported this election, as they could not fail to see that Maraquando would make an exceptionally vigorous and firm-handed President. Though there was no doubt that Don Franicsco had committed suicide out of pique at being deposed from the active command of affairs, yet the Junta, ignoring the manner of his death, and thinking only of his past services, decreed the late President a state funeral.

The houses of the city were draped in black, the flags floated half-mast high, the minute guns boomed at intervals from the forts, and, with all due formalities, President Gomez was interred in the vaults of the Cathedral. When the ceremony was at an end, a weight seemed to be lifted off the city. The bad fortune which had persistently dogged the later months of Don Francisco's rule seemed to be passing away, and, under the vigorous leadership of Maraquando, the capital became wildly patriotic. One idea pervaded the minds of all—that the war was to be ended at once, and that Xuarez was to be crushed by prompt and well-conceived measures.

After the Indians had sacked Chichimec, it was naturally expected that they would march southward and join Don Hypolito before Centeotl. Instead of this, however, the savages began to threaten the capital, and daily bands of well-horsed braves would scour the plains before the Puerta de la Culebra.

Sometimes the soldiers on guard, exasperated by this insolent defiance of the principal city of Cholacaca, would dash out in small parties; but on such a sally being made, the Indians always disappeared. The bulk of their army still lay (as was ascertained by spies) at Chichimec, and it seemed as though these scouting parties were anxious to draw the troops of the Junta from behind the walls, so as to fall on them in the open plain.

President Maraquando was anxious to march his whole army south, and encounter Don Hypolito in the neighbourhood of Centeotl. In order to do this, he would have to overcome the hordes of savages which formed a living barrier between Tlatonac and Chichimec. This entailed some risk. If beaten by the Indians, he would have to fall back on the capital in a crippled condition, and thus give Xuarez time to increase and discipline his army. Then, again, even if he did succeed in conquering these bloodthirsty tribes, he would in all probability lose many of his men, and be forced to encounter Don Hypolito's fresh soldiers with jaded and diminished troops.

At one time he thought of waiting until the return

of the torpederas from Janjalla, and then embarking his troops on *The Iturbide*, proceed southward to attack Xuarez in the rear. Even there the savages would have to be reckoned with, and during his absence, and that of the greater portion of his troops, would perhaps attack the capital. Besides, Maraquando did not wish to risk an expedition to Janjalla unless *The Cortes* were either sunk or captured. Altogether, he was in a state of much perplexity, and the only way by which he could make a move was to detach the Indians from the cause of Xuarez. This task was accomplished by Jack Duval in what seemed to be almost a miraculous fashion.

The new President entertained a great opinion of Duval's abilities. He invariably found him clear-headed and shrewd, capable of giving good advice, and wonderfully prompt in coming to a decision in time of emergency. Therefore, when, shortly after the death of Don Francisco, the young man called to see him at the Casa Maraquando, with a view to lay a certain proposition before him useful to the Republic, Don Miguel interviewed him at once, and gave him his fullest attention.

Some time since, Peter, with Tim's notes, had started in *The Bohemian* for Truxillo, and at the last moment Philip had decided to go with him. Jack desired to confer with Maraquando about his proposed scheme, and to be on the spot in order to carry it out. Tim was afraid to leave the capital lest he should miss some stirring event likely to be of value to his paper; but Philip had no special reason for remaining constantly at Tlatonac, unless for the sake of Doña Eulalia. Dr. Grench did not object to go to Truxillo in *The Bohemian*, but on observing that he would feel more at ease regarding the navigation of the vessel if Philip commanded her, the baronet promptly decided to go. It was a good thing for Peter that old Benker had not heard this reflection on his seamanship, else he would have been much displeased. At all events, Peter, by artfully putting the matter in this light, secured Philip for his companion, and the yacht had departed the previous day for Honduras. She was expected back in four days, and Philip determined on his return voyage to stand in close to the shore of Janjalla, and assure himself of the result of the expedition against *The Cortes*.

Jack made his appearance in the patio in the company of Cocom, whose presence he required in the delicate proposal he had to make. He intended to appeal to the superstitious side of the Indian character, and wanted Cocom to back up his opinion so as to induce Don Miguel to give his consent to an experiment he desired to attempt connected with the harlequin opal. Don Miguel was on the azotea smoking endless cigarettes, and glancing over some papers relating to the Civil Government. His secretary was present, but when Duval appeared, the President sent him below with the documents, and received Jack and his factotum alone. Jack took a seat by the President, and Cocom, rolling a cigarette, squatted on the floor, wrapped in his zarape.

"Where is the Señor Corresponsal?" asked Don Miguel, solemnly, after the first greetings had passed between them.

"At the Puerta de la Culebra," replied Jack, taking the cigar offered to him by the old gentleman. "I asked him to wait there, Señor, as in an hour or so the peon sent by your Excellency to Chichimec is expected back."

"Bueno! But what news do you expect by the peon?"

"News that the Indians contemplate an advance on Tlatonac!"

"Por todos Santos! Don Juan, such a thing cannot be. The Indians would not dare to so insult the majesty of the Republic."

Jack privately thought the majesty of the Republic had been pretty well insulted already, but wisely refrained from giving voice to such an opinion.

"The Indians, Excelencia!" he said, smoothly, "are, according to trustworthy reports, six thousand strong, and thus think themselves a match for even the capital of Cholacaca. They have reduced Puebla de los Naranjos to ashes, they have sacked Chichimec without hindrance, and, excited by such victories, have rashly determined to attack Tlatonac on their own account without waiting for the arrival of Xuarez."

"Do you really think they will dare to camp under our walls?" asked Don Miguel, still incredulous.

"I really do think so, Excelencia," replied Jack, frankly. "If you think I am too rash in pronouncing such an opinion, question our friend Cocom. He has already rendered great services to you and to the Republic. Therefore, you must know that he speaks truth. Speak to him, Señor."

The President turned his eyes towards the old Indian, who, impassive as an idol, sat at his feet smoking a cigarette. He answered Maraquando's inquiring look with a grunt of assent to Jack's remark.

"I am a true Indian, Excelencia! Of the Mayas I am, and my name is that of their kings. Cocom speaks now the truth. Don Xuarez is also an Indian, he comes from the hidden city of Totatzine. He has an understanding with the high-priest, Ixtlilxochitli. Don Hypolito said war, and the Chalchuih Tlatonac, through the priests of Huitzilopochtli, said war. Therefore are six thousand Indians in arms. Now the opal is in the possession of the enemies of the god—in Tlatonac, a city hated by Ixtlilxochitli and Xuarez. They have told their fighting men that this war is a holy war, for the recovery of the sacred shining stone. Were it not for the opal, the Indians would not dare to come to Tlatonac even with six thousand braves. But it is a holy war. They will dare anything to recover the sacred stone. There-

fore will they come here, Excelencia, and camp under
your walls.   This is the truth, I swear by the shrine
of the Holy Mother of God."

"It might be so," said Maraquando, musingly ; "the
opal is in Tlatonac, without doubt.   My niece has it
in her chamber, and knowing how sacred the Indians
hold the gem, I doubt but that they will fight boldly
to gain it again for the hidden shrine of their God,
Huitzilopochtli."

"Assuredly, Don Miguel.   And to gain it they will
come to Tlatonac."

"That must not be!" cried the President, emphatically ; "I will send an army against them, and
encounter their host at Chichimec."

"With what result, Señor ? Even if you conquered,
the victory would cost you many men, and thus
would your army be weakened to encounter Xuarez."

"True, true! Don Juan.   But what then is to be
done."

"Let the Indian army come to Tlatonac.   Let them
camp under the walls.   Close the gates of the city,
and make no hostile sign."

"What say you, Señor?" said Maraquando, in a

fiery tone. "Would you have me leave this savage foe in peace till joined by Don Hypolito—by the rebel Xuarez?"

"They will not be joined by Xuarez, Don Miguel. When the rebels arrive, they will find no savage allies under the walls of Tlatonac."

"If it could be so, it would be well. But how, Señor, do you propose to make this savage army vanish without a blow?"

"By means of the Chalchuih Tlatonac."

"I do not understand, mi amigo. Explain, if you will be so gracious. I am all attention."

Jack began to explain without further preamble.

"Observe, Excelencia," he said slowly, so that Don Miguel could have no difficulty in following his reasons, "It is now noon—this night, if I mistake not, the Indian army will come to Tlatonac—— "

"Bueno!" interrupted Cocom, nodding his head like a mandarin, "I have heard this thing spoken with many tongues. Your messenger, Excelencia, will confirm what I say. The Indian army will march this night for Tlatonac. At dawn will you see them encamped round the walls."

" Proceed, Don Juan," said the President, gravely.

" As you can see, Señor Maraquando," pursued Jack, emphasising his remarks with his finger, " the savages will not arrive till night, so as it is now but noon, we will have time to make ready for their arrival."

" Dios ! You said make no preparations ! "

" Not hostile preparations! No, Señor ; listen, I pray you. We have the Chalchuih Tlatonac, the properties of which are regarded with superstitious reverence by the Indians. What the opal commands they will do. When it glows red, they prepare for war. Let an azure ray shine, and they know that the god commands peace, and, at whatever cost, will lay down their arms."

" How is this done, this glowing of red, of blue ? " •

" I will explain, Señor. In the hidden city I saw it. The opal hung by a golden thread before the shrine of Huitzilopochtli, and this thread was twisted in a certain way by the priests. By careful calculation, they could tell how far it would untwist, so that the opal stone depended motionless, showing the colour they wished. If they desired war, the red side of the stone revealed itself—if peace the blue. To prophesy plenty, the yellow ray came to the front, and so on with all the tints."

"Then you say, Don Juan, that if these Indians saw the opal glowing blue, they would lay down their arms?"

"Assuredly, Señor! and withdraw at once to Totatzine, leaving Xuarez to meet the forces of the Junta alone. If the stone glows blue, they know it is the will of the god that they should not fight."

Don Miguel smiled incredulously.

"I doubt, Señor, whether these warriors, flushed with the sacking of Puebla de los Naranjos and Chichimec would obey the stone now, even though it glowed blue and thus proclaimed peace."

"Excelencia!" broke in Cocom, earnestly, "you know, not the power of the Chalchuih Tlatonac. I, Señor am a good Catholic. I believe not in the devil stone; but my countrymen, Señor, think that the spirit of the god Huitzilopochtli dwells in the gem. They believe that he would punish them with plagues unto death were they to disobey his will as conveyed by the opal. The shining precious stone is the strongest thing in the world to them. Believe me, Excelencia, that when the warriors see the stone glow blue, even were they on the eve of entering Tlatonac, they would lay down their arms and retire to the forests."

"I trust this may be so," said Maraquando, addressing himself to Jack, not unimpressed by the Indian's speech ; "but where, Señor Duval, do you propose to let them see the opal?"

"In the chapel of Padre Ignatius, outside the walls," replied Jack, promptly. "Cocom knows where there is an image of the war-god. He will set it up on the altar of the chapel. Before it, by a thread, we will hang the sacred stone. At dawn all will be ready, and Cocom can so twist the thread that when the opal hangs motionless it will glow blue. The Indians will arrive during the night. At dawn they will spread themselves through the suburbs, and enter the chapel of the good Padre. There they will see the image of their god, the sacred splendour of the opal. They will kneel down and worship, watching the twisting of the gem. When it stops and glows blue, then will they know Huitzilopochtli is satisfied with the sacking of the two towns, and now commands peace. Before noon, Excelencia, there will not be a single Indian left before the walls. They will retire into the forests, to the sacred city of Totatzine, and thus will Xuarez lose his allies."

Maraquando listened to this proposal in silence, his cheek resting in the palm of his right hand, nor when Jack had concluded did he alter his position. He mused long and deeply, neither of his guests attempting to interrupt his meditations. This idea of detaching the Indians from Xuarez, by means of the opal, seemed to him to be childish. That an army of six thousand untutored savages flushed with victory should voluntarily retire at the bidding of Huitzilopochtli spoken through the stone, seemed improbable. But then Maraquando had never been to Totatzine, he did not know in what extreme veneration the opal was held by the Indians, and thus deemed Jack's proposition weak, when in reality it could scarcely have been stronger. Nothing is so powerful as superstition, and to work on the minds of the Indians through their abject belief in the virtues of the shining precious stone was a masterstroke on the part of Duval.

" It seems to me," said Maraquando, at length

raising his eyes, " that the carrying out of this scheme will entail the loss of the opal."

" Without doubt, Señor," replied Duval, coolly ; "but by such a sacrifice you gain more than you lose. The Indians will desert Xuarez, you will be able to march your army south, and conquer him in the neighbourhood of Centeotl before he has time to approach nearer to the capital. Then you can crush his nest of traitors in Acauhtzin. Better lose the opal than Tlatonac, and if we do not succeed in getting rid of the Indians it may be that the city will fall."

" What says my niece Doña Dolores ? "

" I have spoken to her, Señor, and for the sake of the city, she is willing to run the risk of losing the jewel."

Don Miguel smiled approvingly. He was patriotic himself, and liked to see the same quality displayed by all his family. At the same time, he was a just man, and knowing how Dolores loved the gem, did not care about taking advantage of her offer to sacrifice the same, unless she voluntarily consented to surrender the sacred stone.

" We will ask the lady herself," he said, rising from

his chair. "One moment, Señor; I shall return with my niece."

He disappeared down the staircase leading to the patio, and Jack was left alone with Cocom.

"It may be that the Indians will not dare to take the jewel," said Jack, looking at the old man.

Cocom uttered a grunt which might have meant anything.

"Rest content, Don Juan. Once the Chalchuih Tlatonac leaves the walls of the city, it will never return again. Back to the sacred shrine of Totatzine shall it go. The high priest has ordered it be sought for far and wide, lest the god afflict the people with plagues for its loss."

"Still, if I remained in the chapel, and watched it."

"You, Señor? Nay, that, indeed, would be rash, The Indians would slay you. Only one will watch the jewel; but that one cannot prevent the worshippers seizing it."

"You mean yourself?"

"It is said. I speak of Cocom. He shall sit by the image of the god, when the Indians enter the chapel of the good father."

" But the Indians might slay you, Cocom."

"That which is to be must be," replied the old man, stolidly. "Cocom must watch the sacred gem, so that it sends the blue ray of peace from its breast. The tribes have been told by Ixtlilxochitli that Cocom is a traitor, and false to the worship of the old gods. When he is seen, he must die."

" But my friend, I——"

" Be silent, Señor. Not you nor any man can turn aside the spear of Teoyamiqui. Why should I murmur if death be my portion ? I am old, I am mutilated, I am weary of life. If I die I die, and for the safety of the white people. It may be, Señor, that, as says the good Padre, Cocom shall go to the heaven of the Christians. With the Virgin such going rests."

Jack found no words to reply to this speech, and remained silently thinking of how he could save the old man from death. He had as yet arrived at no conclusion, when Don Miguel appeared with his niece on the floor of the azotea. Dolores ran towards Jack and threw herself into his arms.

" Querido," she said in a tender voice, " my good uncle tells me of your scheme. It is that of which you spoke to me. It may save Tlatonac from savage foes, and thus do I aid you to the extent of my powers."

She held out the opal towards him.

"You may lose it altogether, Dolores."

"No matter, Juanito. It may save the city."

"And you consent to this sacrifice, Don Miguel?"

"Yes, Señor. I think it will turn aside this host of savages. With them away, we can hope to conquer Xuarez. Otherwise——" Maraquando stopped suddenly, and made a gesture of despair.

"Of course it is merely an experiment," said Jack, doubtfully.

"But one which must be successful," cried Dolores, quickly. "Querido, can you doubt that, after what we saw in the sacred city? As the god speaks through the opal, so will the Indians act. Let it dart, then, its blue ray, and drive them back to their forests."

"You are sure you can make it shine blue, Cocom?"

"Señor," said the old man, with great dignity, "I give my life to prove that this shall be so."

Jack took the opal from the outstretched hand of Dolores.

"So be it!" he cried, fervently. "The opal has

brought the Indians to Tlatonac ; the opal shall send them back again to Totatzine."

Tim suddenly made his appearance with a face full of excitement.

" Jack ! Señor Maraquando ! " he said, quickly, in Spanish, " the messenger you sent to spy on the Indians at Chichimec has returned."

" What does he say, Señor Corresponsal ? "

" That the whole host of Indians are marching from Chichimec, and will be camped round the walls at dawn. Dios ! We are lost ! "

" No," cried Jack, brightly, " we are saved ! "

" What the deuce will save us, Jack ? " asked Tim, in English.

" This ! "

Duval held up the harlequin opal. A ray of sunlight struck the jewel, and a blue ray darted out like a tongue of steel.

"Bueno ! " said Cocom, stolidly, " the Chalchuih Tlatonac prophesies peace."

CHAPTER VI.

THE LUCK OF THE OPAL.

The red ray dies in the opal stone,
The god hath spoken,
Arrow and bow and spear be broken,
Red of war is the fiery token,
And lo ! in the zone,
It pales, and fades, and faints, and dies,
As sunsets wane in the eastern skies.

The blue ray glows in the opal's heart,
The god is smiling,
Victims no more need we be piling,
On altar stone for his dread beguiling ;
The blue rays dart
To tell us war must surely cease,
So in the land let there be peace.

JACK at once proceeded to execute his project. Fortunately Padre Ignatius had gone south in *The Iturbide*, thinking his ministrations might be required by
the wounded, else Duval would never have gained
the good priest's consent to such a desecration of his
chapel. As it was, Jack hoped to carry out his

scheme, and restore the chapel to its original state before the return of the old man. The actual elevation of a heathen idol on the shrine of the Virgin, not being seen by Padre Ignatius, he would think less of the sacrilegious act, more especially when he would find on his return the altar in nearly the same state as when he left it. Being a Protestant, Jack had no scruples about the matter, and Cocom was such a queer mixture of paganism and Catholicism, that his views were not very decided. He believed in the Virgin certainly; but seeing that her altar was required to save the city, Cocom thought that she surely would not object to the conversion for a time of her chapel into a heathen temple. Besides, if this was not done, the Indians would be sure to destroy the shrine, so it was best to make an attempt to avert such a disaster, even in such an illegitimate way, rather than risk the whole place being destroyed by the savages. This was Cocom's idea in the matter, therefore he proceeded to put an image of Huitzilopochtli in the place occupied by the cross. Father Ignatius would have died of horror had he witnessed such daring.

All the afternoon they laboured to transfer the chapel into a semblance of the temple of the war-god, and at length succeeded in making it a very fair representation. Huitzilopochtli, his left foot decked with humming-bird feathers, was set up on the shrine itself, a small altar on which a fire was lighted burned before him, and the walls were draped with mats of featherwork and pictured linen, whereon were depicted the hideous forms of Aztec deities. From the roof, by a golden thread, hung the famous opal, spinning in the dim light. After some calculation, Cocom made a hole in the roof of the chapel, so that when the sun rose over the walls of the city his beams would pour through the opening and bathe the gem in floods of gold.

Where Cocom had discovered all this idolatrous paraphernalia Jack could not make out, nor would the old Indian tell. But it confirmed Duval in his belief that in the near neighbourhood of Tlatonac the natives still worshipped the gods of their ancestors, for the celerity with which Cocom had produced statue, pictured linen, and altar, pointed to the existence of some hidden temple close at hand. In fact, despite Cocom's asseverations to the contrary, Jack began to be doubtful as to his really being a Christian, for he betrayed far too much knowledge of paganism in its worst form to be quite orthodox. One thing, however, was certain, that, pagan or not, Cocom was greatly incensed against Ixtlilxochitli for maiming him, and was doing his best to thwart the plans of the savage old priest.

Things having been thus arranged, towards sunset Jack tried to persuade Cocom to return with him to the city, and leave the opal to work out its own spell. This the obstinate octogenarian refused to do, averring that without his personal superintendence the scheme would fail. Jack unwilling that a man from whom he had derived so many benefits should be left unprotected amid a horde of bloodthirsty savages, insisted on remaining with him to keep vigil during the night. This offer Cocom also refused, and implored Jack to return at once to the city, and have the gates closed, as it was near sunset, and the Indian army would soon be close at hand.

" Leave me here, Señor," he said, with quiet

obstinacy. "It may be that I fall not into their hands. They may take the opal—that is sure—but they may not take me. If you remain, your white skin will attract their fury, and they may sacrifice you before that very altar you have assisted to rear. I am an Indian, a Maya. Dog does not bite dog. It may be that I shall escape."

"Not if Ixtlilxochitli can help it."

"Oh, that evil one! He would have my blood, I know, Don Juan. But behold, Señor, if I—as the Indians, my countrymen, think—took the opal from Totatzine, I now bring it back again. That may save me!"

"But, Cocom—— "

"Depart, Señor; I have my own plans. What says the proverb of the white people? 'Every one is master of his own soul.' Go! I save mine as I will!"

It seemed to Jack that Cocom was desirous of wearing the crown of martyrdom. However, it was useless to turn him from his purpose, as he was obstinately set on daring the fury of the Indians. Jack, for a moment, thought of employing force, and looked at the spare frame of the old man, with the idea of picking him up and bearing him inside the city. Perhaps something of his purpose showed itself in his eyes, for Cocom suddenly darted out of the chapel and disappeared. Though he searched everywhere, Jack was unable to find him, so proceeded to the Puerta de la Culebra, and reported his arrival to Don Sebastian, who was stationed there in command of the guard.

"And the Indian, Señor?"

"Refuses to come within, Don Sebastian. He says he is safe outside."

De Ahumada shrugged his shoulders, and made the same remark as had Cocom some quarter of an hour before.

"Bueno! Dog does not bite dog."

Then he ordered the gates to be closed, which was accordingly done. It was now too late to alter existing circumstances, and the whole chances of detaching the Indian host from the cause of Xuarez lay with Cocom and the opal. Jack went off to the Casa Maraquando, in order to inform Don Miguel of all that had been done, and then rewarded himself for that wearisome afternoon by chatting with Dolores. It had been deemed advisable, by Don Miguel, to keep Jack's scheme secret, lest, should the attempt fail, and the opal be lost, the populace should lose heart in the forthcoming struggle with Xuarez. So long as the opal was in the city, they deemed themselves invincible; so, whether the attempt to detach the Indians succeeded or failed, Maraquando determined that the people of Tlatonac should still think that the sacred stone was in the possession of his niece.

Late that night Jack went on the walls with Tim, and together they watched the Indians gather round the walls. Above the Puerta de la Culebra was fixed a powerful electric light, which irradiated a considerable portion of the space beyond the gate. Without the walls there was quite a town, as the huts of the peons stretched away in long lines, alternating with palms, cacti, aloes, and densely foliaged ombú trees. Close to the gate these huts clustered thickly together, but after a time became scattered, and finally ceased on the verge of the plains, where the ground was thickly covered with brushwood.

The Indians, fearful of the guns protruding from

the walls, and doubtful of the weird glare of the
electric light, kept away beyond the line of huts, and
finally camped in the open ground beyond. Not-
withstanding the distance they kept from the town
the powerful rays of electric light blazed full on
their camp, and caused them considerable uneasiness.
The two Englishmen could see their tall, dark forms,
gliding like ghosts through the white radiance, and at
times a mounted troop of horsemen would dash
furiously across the circle of light, disappearing into
the further darkness. Just below, a stone's throw
from the wall, arose the little chapel of Father
Ignatius, beneath whose roof Cocom, with the opal,
awaited the dawn.

For some hours Jack watched the strange sight
that savage picture, starting out of the surrounding
darkness, and ultimately retired to his house, hopeful
that before noon of the next day all the Indians
would have disappeared. Tim remained behind, talking to Don Sebastian, and scribbling notes in his
book; but at last he also went to rest, and the wall
was left in possession of De Ahumada and his guard.
All night long the electric light flashed its beams on

the camp, so as to guard against an unexpected attack by the Indians.

At dawn, the savages were up and doing before sunrise. They gathered together in groups, and talked of how they were to attack this formidable city, whose colossal walls bid defiance to their puny weapons. They could see soldiers moving along the ramparts, the black muzzles of the guns frowning fiercely down, and wondered at the absolute indifference of the Republic, who thus permitted her hereditary enemies to camp before the gates of her principal city. Everything within the town was quiet, the gates were firmly closed, no peons were to be seen moving about the suburbs, and the Indians, blackening the plain with their thousands of men and horses stood perplexed before this intensely silent town.

The east was flaming redly over the ocean waves. The Indians could see the long line of battlements black against the clear crimson sky. No wind blew across the desert, and the great banner of the opal hung motionless from its tall staff. Suddenly, in the red sky, a yellow beam shot up into the cold blue of the zenith ; another and another followed, spreading like a gigantic fan. The savages threw themselves on their knees, and held up their hands in supplication to the great deity, who was even now being invoked with sacrifice in the hidden town of Totatzine.

The gold of the sky seemed to boil up behind the walls of the town, as though it would run over in yellow streams. Then the dazzling orb appeared, and fierce arrows shot across the green suburbs to the sandy desert, where those thousands of naked Indians were kneeling. Suddenly a man started in surprise, and looked inquiringly at his companions. They listened as he had done, and also looked astonished. In a miraculously short space of time the whole host were in a state of commotion. Those in front stood still in a listening attitude, those behind pressed forward to hear this miracle which had startled their companions. Loud and shrill arose the song from the chapel of Padre Ignatius. It was the hymn of the opal daily chaunted by the priests of Huitzilopochtli in the city of Totatzine.

The chiefs hastily gathered together, and consulted as to the meaning of this prodigy. Never before had the sacred song been heard beyond the shrine of the sacred city, and now its music was thrilling through the still morning air under the very walls of the capital. The mystery must be solved at any cost, and commanding their warriors to wait in the camp, all five chiefs, the leaders of the host, flung themselves on their horses, and galloped bravely up to the chapel. It was a dangerous thing to do, for at any moment those terrible guns might vomit forth fire and death ; but the chiefs did not care. Fanaticism, dread of the gods, was their most powerful characteristic, and dismounting from their horses, they entered the door of the chapel whence the chaunt of the opal proceeded.

At the entrance they stood transfixed with surprise, and for the moment deemed they were in the Shrine of the Opal at Totatzine. Half-veiled by clouds of white smoke rolling upward from a small altar, they could see the terrible features of Huitzilopochtli, in all his blood-stained glory. The mats of feather-work hung glittering from the walls ; they marked the grotesque visages of their deities scowling from pictured walls, and behind the altar, the hidden minstrel chaunted the hymn of the opal.

The opal! There it hung in the centre of the white smoke. A ray of golden light, like a finger from heaven, smote it with terrible glory. It was turning rapidly, as they had seen it in the temple of the god at Totatzine.

"Chalchuih Tlatonac!" they cried, and all five prostrated themselves before the sacred gem. High and shrill rang out the song from the hidden singer, and the chiefs, with reverential awe, watched the spinning opal. Red, yellow, blue, green, the rays flashed out jets of many-coloured fire every second. It began to revolve more slowly. Slower and slower! a pause!—it hung motionless, and a ray of azure shone benignly from its breast.

The song ceased, and a tall man, arrayed in white garments, came from behind the shrine, holding a blue cloak full length in his arms. This was the ritual prescribed at the shrine of Huitzilopochtli when the god spoke through the opal.

"The god proclaims peace!"

His voice broke the spell. The Indians dashed forward, and strove to seize him, but he eluded their grip, and vanished.

" Peace ! Peace ! Peace !" they heard him cry three times. Their attention was fixed on the opal, and they did not pursue him.

" The sacred stone !" cried the supreme chief ; " we must bear it back to the shrine of the god Forgive us, oh, holy one."

He snapped the stone off the string, and darted out of the door, followed by his four companions. At the door an old Indian, now divested of his sacerdotal garments, met them, and rushed on their principal with a cry of anger.

" The opal ! Give me back the sacred gem ! "

" Cocom !" cried the chief, raising his tomahawk. " It was thou who thieved the gem ! Die, vile wretch, who desecrated the shrine of the god."

His companions restrained his wrath. The fear of the opal was on them.

" Nay, Tezuco. The god says peace ! The stone burns blue rays."

" Bind him, then, and we will take him to Totatzine ; there to be sacrificed on the altar of the offended god."

In a moment Cocom, in spite of his struggles, was

thrown across the back of the horse of one of the chiefs, and they all rode off rapidly towards the camp. In the centre of the throng, Tezuco halted, and held up his hand. Therein flashed the opal, and a cry of delight arose from the host, who in a moment recognised the gem, and at once prostrated themselves before its glory.

"Children of the war-god. This hath been given to us again. We saw the stone revolve—we saw it stay. Blue was the ray of the gem. Blue, my children, is the sign of peace. Huitzilopochtli, the lord of war, is appeased. He proclaims peace. No longer wait we here. To Totatzine !"

"To Totatzine !" roared the vast host, and, at a signal, rushed for their horses. War, plunder, Xuarez, all was forgotten. The blue ray of the opal proclaimed peace, and this vast host, laying down its arms, departed at the bidding of the god.

The townspeople on the walls of the city saw with amazement the Indians suddenly, without any apparent reason, strike their camp, and file off in long lines towards the north. Astonished at the sight, Don Sebastian sent off a message to the President.

In a quarter of an hour he arrived at the Puerta de la Culebra, followed by Jack and Tim.

"Behold, Señor!" cried Jack, triumphantly pointing to the myriads tramping across the plain. "Did I not speak truly? The opal has done its work."

"The opal! The opal!" murmured those around him, and the cry being caught up by the populace, passed from one mouth to another. The crowd on the walls, seeing in the departure of the Indians the influence of the opal, began to cry out madly. They deemed that the opal was still within the walls of Tlatonac.

"Viva el opale! El Chalchuih Tlatonac!"

"Bueno!" said Maraquando, with satisfaction, shaking Jack by the hand; "you were right, Señor. The Indians will give us no more trouble. Now we can crush Xuarez in the south. Señor de Ahumada open the gates!"

In a few moments His Excellency, followed by Jack Tim, and Don Sebastian, was galloping in the direction of the chapel. They reached it, dismounted, and entered. The opal was gone and Cocom also!

"I knew we would lose the opal," said Jack, cheer-

fully; " but I thought they would kill Cocom. Fortunately they have only taken him prisoner."

"To reserve him for a more cruel death in Totatzine,
Señor," replied Maraquando, his delight slightly
damped. "He has served the Republic well. I would
he could have been saved."

" Poor devil!" murmured Tim, in English, as they
remounted their horses. " In any case, Jack, his death
has saved the Republic. Now the savages have gone
away, it won't be difficult to thrash Don Hypolito."

At the city gates a new surprise awaited them. Don
Rafael, mounted on a mustang, came galloping through
the gate, and reined up his steed in front of his astonished father.

" My father! Great news; good news! I have just
returned in *The Montezuma*. We have captured *The
Cortes* and the transports."

Don Miguel looked incredulous. This news,
coming after the departure of the Indians, seemed too
good to be true.

" It is true, my father," said Rafael, proudly. " By
noon to-day you will see them in the harbour. Now
Don Hypolito has no fleet."

Hurrah !" cried Jack, tossing his hat in the air. " The luck of the opal ! "

Those near repeated his exclamation. It swelled into a roar, and throughout Tlatonac only one cry could be heard, " Vive el opale."

CHAPTER VII.

UNDER THE OPAL FLAG.

Marching away; joyous and gay,
Rank upon rank with a splendid display,
Leaving the city at breaking of day.

Riding along, gallant and strong,
Round us the populace tearfully throng,
Greeting our going with patriot's song.

Under our feet, flower-buds sweet;
Tread we in marching through plaza and street,
Never our kinsfolk again may we meet.

Laurels to earn; foemen to spurn;
Only for glory we anxiously yearn,
Conquerors all we will hither return.

"JUAN," said Dolores, seriously, "I believe the opal brought us bad fortune. While it was in the city, Janjalla fell, Don Francisco died, and all went wrong. Now it is lost, the Indians have departed, the fleet of Xuarez is destroyed, and everything promises well for the future."

"That is true, in one sense, yet wrong in another,"

VOL. III.   I replied Jack, smiling. "You must not forget that it was through the opal the Indians departed, and while it was in Tlatonac, *The Pizarro* was sunk, and the two other warships captured."

"I suppose never again shall I behold the opal, Juanito?"

"Not unless you care to pay a second visit to Totatzine."

Dolores shuddered. The memory of their peril in the hidden city was a painful one. Recent events had not obliterated the recollection of that terrible journey to the coast through the tropical forest.

"I would certainly not care about seeing Totatzine again, querido. And yet I would—if only to save Cocom!"

"It is impossible to save Cocom," responded Jack, a trifle sadly. "The only way to do so would be to lead an army to the hidden city, and rescue him. But how can such a thing be done in that narrow, secret way? Our soldiers would be cut to pieces in those rocky defiles."

"There is no other way, I suppose?"

"I am not sure, Dolores. That cañon road leads to

the outer world. If we could only enter the valley where Totatzine is built by that way, we might succeed in capturing the city; but I am afraid such an entrance will never be discovered."

"Ay di mi. Then poor Cocom is lost."

"It is his own fault, querida. I tried to save him; but he refused to obey my orders. Still, there is one chance of aiding him, though I am afraid but a faint one."

"And that, my Juan?"

"Listen, angelito! The sacrifice of the cycle does not take place for two months. I have escaped it, but Cocom may now be selected by Ixtlilxochitli as the victim. If we can crush Xuarez and finish the war within the next few weeks, it may be that we can march troops to the sacred city, and save his life."

"But how can you get to the city? By the secret way?"

"No; by the cañon road. See, Dolores! I have an idea!"

They were sitting on the azotea, two days after the Indians had retreated from Tlatonac. Rafael had just left them, full of glee at the proposed expedition to Janjalla, and it was then that Dolores had made the remark about the opal which lead to the conversation regarding Cocom, Totatzine, and the cañon road.

In her lap Dolores had a pile of flowers, which she was arranging for the use of the house. Jack took a handful of these, and, kneeling down on the floor of the azotea, proceeded to illustrate his theory by constructing a map with the blossoms.

"Behold, my own!" he said, deftly placing a bud here and there, "this rose is Totatzine, situate fifty miles from the coast in a straight line. Here is Tlatonac, indicated by this scarlet verbena. From the point where we embarked in the canoe to the capital is twenty miles."

"I understand," said Dolores, much interested in this explanation.

"From Totatzine to the point where we embarked, and from thence to Tlatonac, is what we call a right angle. Now, if I draw a straight line from the capital in a slanting direction, you can see that it passes through Totatzine."

"I see that, querido! but the third line is longer than the other two."

" It is longer than each of the other two lines if you take them separately. Shorter if you take them together. You do not know Euclid, Dolores, else you would discover that any two sides of a triangle are together greater than the third side."

" Wait a moment, Juanito!" exclaimed Dolores, vivaciously. " From Totatzine to the point where we embarked is fifty miles, from thence to Tlatonac twenty miles—in all, seventy miles. But by your reasoning this third line is not seventy miles."

" Of course not! Still I believe it is quite seventy miles from Tlatonac to Totatzine by this new way."

" How so ?"

" Because we cannot go thither in a straight line. If we went by this one I have drawn, the distance would be much shorter than by the secret way of the sea. But as we have to follow the railway it is a longer journey—quite seventy miles. See! This is Cuavaca, at the foot of Xicotencatl—thirty miles from Tlatonac ; from Cuavaca to the terminus of the railway it is twenty miles ; from thence to Totatzine possibly another twenty—in all seventy miles. So you see that the distance each way, owing to the configuration of the country, is precisely the same."

"Yes ; but what of that ?"

"Can you not see ?   At the point where the railway stops it is only twenty miles to Totatzine. Now, if, as I suspect, there is a road leading up the cañon to the city, the distance from the termination of the rail-way works to that road cannot be very far. If, there-fore, we discover the hidden road, we can take our troops up by rail, march the rest of the distance, and enter Totatzine through the mouth of the cañon."

"Oh !" cried Dolores, astonished at this idea. "And you propose to attempt this entrance ?"

"If it can be found. Unfortunately Cocom is the only Indian who could supply such information, and he is a prisoner to Ixtlilxochitli."

"But if he knew of this cañon road, why did he not lead us by that way instead of towards the coast ?"

"You forget the whole country is overrun by Indians. We could not have disguised ourselves as pilgrims had we gone by the cañon road. That is evidently the secular path. The other way to the coast is sacred."

"It might be done, Juanito."

"Yes; but it cannot be done till Xuarez is conquered and the war is ended."

"Santissima!" sighed Dolores, sadly; "and when will that be?"

"Very shortly. Now we have succeeded in getting rid of the Indians, we shall be able to crush Xuarez at one blow."

"When do you march south?"

"To-morrow at the latest."

"Will Señor Felipe be back?"

"No, I am afraid not. In three days I expect the yacht will return. By that time who knows but what we may not have conquered the rebels?"

Shortly afterwards this conversation came to an abrupt conclusion as Don Miguel sent a special messenger to call Jack to the Palacio Nacional. In those days Jack was a very important personage. Maraquando was so impressed by the way in which the Indians had been dealt with that he entertained a higher opinion than ever of Duval's capabilities, and frequently appealed to him for advice. Nor did this create any jealousy, for the Cholacacans were now beginning to regard Duval as one of themselves. He was going to marry the niece of their President; he was the engineer who had constructed the railway; he was deeply interested in the future of the Republic; so it was generally supposed that when the war was at an end he would be naturalized, a citizen of Cholacaca, and take up his abode there altogether. A clever, brilliant young man like Jack was a distinct acquisition to the country, and the liberal-minded Cholacacans welcomed him accordingly.

From the deepest despair the city had passed into a state of great elation. With the death of Gomez, all the bad fortune of the Republic seemed to have vanished. Since Maraquando had seated himself in the Presidential chair, all had gone well, and the superstitious Tlatonacians looked upon him as a ruler likely to bring good fortune to the Republic. Nor was such a belief to be wondered at, seeing how suddenly the tide of fortune had turned within the last few days in favour of the governmental party.

The Indians had departed, and thus was Don Hypolito deprived at one swoop of half his power. *The Cortes* menaced by the *The Columbus, The Iturbide* and the torpederas had surrendered, and now with the transports were lying in the harbour of the capital. Xuarez, by the loss of his fleet, was cut off completely from the north, and shut up in Janjalla with but six thousand troops.

After these events had transpired, the Junta met in the hall of the Palacio Nacional to map out the coming campaign. The whole of the members were on the side of Maraquando. Before the peril which threatened the Republic in the south all party differences had disappeared, and the representatives of the several provinces united in upholding the policy of Don Miguel. This judicious unity was the salvation of the Republic.

The capital was garrisoned by ten thousand troops plentifully supplied with cannon, ammunition, and rifles. This force was under the command of General Benito, who had been elevated to the command after the death of the ill-fated Gigedo at Janjalla. The troops were in a great state of excitement, as it was well known that they were no longer to be held back within the walls of the capital. Maraquando had decided to throw forward nine thousand men as far as Centeotl, and leaving one thousand to defend

Tlatonac, try conclusions with the rebels in the open plains.

At the second conference of the Junta, this decision was somewhat modified by the advice of Benito. That astute commander pointed out that in Janjalla lay the strength of Xuarez. If he was defeated at Centeotl, he could fall back on the southern capital, whereas, if that was in the power of the Government, he would have no chance of retreat, and be thus crushed at one blow. The main thing, therefore, was to capture Janjalla, and deprive the rebels of this last refuge in case of defeat.

It was Rafael who supported the General, and proposed a plan by which the southern city could be taken.

" Señores," cried Rafael, vehemently, " what General Benito says is true. We must leave Xuarez no refuge. He must be crushed between our armies in the north and south. Behold, Señores, in the harbour of our city lie two warships taken from the enemy, now manned by faithful sailors of the Junta. Also the armed cruiser *Iturbide*, and the two torpedo-boats *Zuloaga* and *Montezuma*, one of which I have the honour of commanding. Give us, Señores, the order to steam south. Put two thousand troops on board of the transports. Then we will lie in the harbour of Janjalla, and bombard the town. As Don Hypolito has probably gone north with the bulk of his army to Centeotl, the town will be ill defended. In the end it must surrender, and then we can land our troops and push forward to gain the rear of the rebels. From the north, Señores, seven thousand men will march under the command of General Benito. Thus Xuarez will find himself between two armies, and be forced to surrender or submit to be cut to pieces. The rebels will be defeated and the war will be ended."

This proposition commended itself to the Junta, and was ultimately adopted. At once the fleet, under the command of Captain Pedraza, was sent south, with instructions to bombard and capture Janjalla. Then to lead the troops and push forward to effect a conjunction with General Benito at Centeotl. The warships, the cruiser, torpederas, and transports, left the harbour of the capital that afternoon amid great excitement, and then the populace rolled from sea-gate to land-gate in order to witness the departure of the army for the south.

As yet *The Bohemian* had not returned from Truxillo, a delay which vexed Tim mightily, as he wanted to send the boat off again with fresh despatches. Besides, he knew that Philip would be annoyed at missing the battle which was to decide the fate of the war. When he had left for Truxillo, there had been no chance of the loyalists and rebels meeting in open battle; but of late events had developed so rapidly that it was impossible to delay matters further. The army was marching for Centeotl, and Philip was absent at Truxillo.

Only one person was pleased at this. Eulalia was afraid of losing her lover in what promised to be a terribly sanguinary affair, and was therefore pleased that he was out of danger. She had not the Spartan spirit of her cousin, who, though downcast at the prospect of being separated from Jack, yet bade him march forward with the army to conquer the rebels, and made no attempt to detain him by her side.

Two thousand infantry had embarked on board

the transports for Janjalla, and now the army, consisting of five thousand foot and two thousand horse, left for the front by the Puerta de la Culebra. Maraquando was nominally Commander-in-Chief of the forces, but, his presence being required at Tlatonac, he left the conduct of the campaign to General Benito. The army of Janjalla, proceeding thither by sea, was commanded by Colonel Palo, and he was directed, when the southern city was captured, to march to Centeotl, and effect, if possible, a junction with the troops from the north. There were also forty field-guns, and a battery of gatlings, with a corps of engineers. Thus provided, the army of the Government deemed themselves invincible.

When they set out, Maraquando solemnly delivered to Benito the great standard of the opal, which had never before left the walls of the capital. Now, in all its splendour, it floated over the heads of the soldiers, a shining star, with its glitter of feather-work and jewels, leading them south to victory. With that standard the army could scarcely conceive that there was any chance of defeat.

All signs of the Indians had disappeared. There

was no doubt that, obeying the opal, they had retired
to the sacred city, and there delivered the recovered
treasure to the high priest.   Doubtless Ixtlilxochitli,
still desirous of aiding Xuarez, would stir them up to
war ; but before they could again emerge from the
forests, General Benito hoped to cut the army of Don
Hypolito to pieces, reduce the south to order, and
then marching north, defeat the savage forces under
the walls of the capital.   The great strength of the
Republic lay in the fact that by strategy they had
succeeded in isolating Xuarez in the south.   Owing
to the loss of his fleet, he could no longer depend
upon help from Acauhtzin, and now that his Indian
allies had deserted him, he was forced to meet the
Royalist army with a comparatively small army.

On Monday afternoon the transports, filled with
troops, and convoyed by the warships, left for
Janjalla, and at dawn on Wednesday the army began
to march out of the Puerta de la Culebra on its way
to the south.   Jack took a fond farewell of Dolores,
and soothed her with promises of his speedy return.
Don Miguel, with some members of the Junta, accom-
panied Benito some miles on his way, and then

returned to the capital to wait the upshot of this bold attempt to end the war at a single blow.

From Tlatonac the army marched to Chichimec, which they found in ruins. Hardly a soul was left in the town, for those who survived the massacre had fled southward to Puebla de los Naranjos. It was true that there, also, they would find but ruins. This they did not know, as the telegraph-wires had been cut by the Indians, but as those savages were between Chichimec and the capital, the unfortunate towns-people were only able to escape southward.

Leaving Chichimec, Benito marched to Puebla de los Naranjos, and there found a considerable num-ber of fugitives from the former city. He was in-formed that Centeotl still held out against the rebels, though Xuarez was besieging it hotly, and that Hermanita was untouched by either savage or rebel. This news was very comforting, and desirous of reaching that town by nightfall, the General pushed forward his troops by forced marches. By eight o'clock the army came in sight of Hermanita, and were joyfully greeted by its citizens, who threw open their gates to receive these whom they justly regarded as their deliverers. That night the troops occupied the town.

Centeotl was but twenty miles further on, and Benito was desirous of ascertaining the position of Xuarez before venturing to give battle. He sent out Indian spies, and these speedily brought reports as to the numerical strength of the rebels. It appeared that Xuarez had in all about seven thousand troops, as he had been joined by several of the smaller towns of the Republic. He had left but five hundred to garrison Janjalla, never for a moment dreaming that, guarded as was the town by *The Cortes*, it would be attacked by the loyalists from the sea. Now having lost his sole remaining warship, he could not help seeing that his position was desperate. By his spies, he learned that the army under Benito was camped at Hermanita, and that Janjalla was being bombarded by the fleet of the Junta.

At one time he thought of falling back on Janjalla, concentrating all his force within its walls, and holding out against the loyalists, until reinforced by his Indian allies. As yet he knew not that they had deserted him and withdrawn to their forests. Had he been aware of his isolated position, he might have come to terms with the Junta, but relying on the aid of the savages, and trusting to Ixtlilxochitli's promises, he felt confident that he would gain a victory. As Janjalla was being bombarded by the warships, he decided not to fall back there, as he would but expose his troops to a double danger : the land army of Benito and the bombs from the sea.

What he proposed to do was to meet Benito at Centeotl, defeat his army, and then either occupy that town, and hold out till his allies came south, or march north to effect a conjunction with them before the capital. As to Janjalla, he could do nothing to relieve it. It was absolutely necessary that he should keep his troops together, so as to meet the army of the Republic under Benito. Before Janjalla fell into the hands of the Junta, he hoped to conquer the land forces. It was all a chance, and he fully recognised that his position was most perilous. The only hope he had of turning the tide of fortune in his favour was to be joined by the Indians from the north.

The warships had left Tlatonac on Monday afternoon, and General Benito, knowing the weak garrison at Janjalla, calculated that the city would succumb to the bombardment by Friday at the latest. It was now the morning of that day, and he determined to march his troops forward to meet the rebel army. From Janjalla, from Hermanita to Centeotl, it was but twenty miles each way; and assuming that Janjalla was captured, as there was every reason to believe, General Benito hoped that the two thousand troops from the south, and his own forces from the north would meet at Centeotl about the same time.

With this idea, he marched with his full strength to Centeotl, for now that the Indians had vanished, he had no fear of being attacked in the rear, and if forced to retreat, could fall back on Hermanita, that city being defended by its ordinary garrison. Don Hypolito, so as not to expose his troops to the double fire of town and plain, left the shelter of the walls, and occupied a low range of hillocks running at right angles from the city. Between him and Benito flowed the river broad and sluggish.

By noon the armies faced one another. At one o'clock the first shot was fired, and the battle of Centeotl began.

CHAPTER VIII.

THE BATTLE OF CENTEOTL.

The squadrons move across the plain,
Beneath a rain
Of deadly missiles falling, falling.
Oh, could we gain
Those heights beyond, where guns are calling,
Of deeds appalling,
One to the other not in vain,
Then might we conquer in the fray,
And victors be e'er close of day.

THE stream lying between the two armies was called the Rio Tardo, from its slow-flowing current, and emerging from the interior mountains, pursued its way in many windings to the sea. Centeotl was built on the left bank, so that the loyalists were unable to occupy the town without crossing the river, and to do so they would have had to force a passage at the point of the sword. The battle took place about three miles from the city, on a large plain streaked here and there with low ranges of sandy

K 2

hills, and intersected by the broad stream of the Rio
Tardo.

On one of these ranges Don Hypolito had planted
his artillery, and swept the river with his heavy guns.
He also disposed his infantry along the banks, whence
they kept up a regular fire of musketry on the loyalists. The bridge at Centeotl had been destroyed
prior to the arrival of Benito, so that there was no way
of crossing, save under fire from the foot soldiers,
or in the teeth of the battery posted on the sandy
ridges.

Behind this battery Xuarez held his cavalry in
reserve, lest the loyalists should accomplish the passage of the river, and the combatants come to closer
quarters. Between Centeotl and the position he had
taken up, he placed a line of some thousand horse,
with the object of preventing an attack by the besieged in his rear. In the disposition of his troops,
he showed a wonderful skill in taking advantage of
the capabilities of the ground, and General Benito saw
plainly that it would be with considerable difficulty
that he could effect a crossing of the Rio Tardo.

On his side there were no ranges of hills upon

which he could post his artillery, or by which he could protect his men. Nothing but a desolate plain covered with brushwood incapable of offering the least shelter against the devastating fire of the insurgents. His only way of crossing the river was to silence the battery on the sandhills. With this object, he brought up his field-guns, and opened a heavy cannonade on the heights beyond. The rebels replied, and for over two hours this cross fire went on without intermission on either side. Benito trusted by this gunnery to deceive the insurgents as to his real purpose, which was to attempt a crossing with five hundred horse three miles further up the stream, near the ruins of the bridge. By doing so he could take Xuarez in the rear, and while the rebels were employed in facing this new danger from an unexpected quarter, hoped to cross the river with his full force.

Don Hypolito evidently suspected this stratagem, for he kept a sharp eye on the disposition of the loyalist army in the direction of Centeotl. When he saw a body of horse move citywards to effect a crossing, he at once sent a troop of cavalry to dispute the passage,

Benito seeing this, despatched a battery of six gatlings to support his troops, trusting that under the cover of these guns playing on the enemy they could force the stream. At once Xuarez brought up his field-artillery, and in a short space of time the cannonading lower down the river was being repeated further up at the ruins of the bridge.

The right wing of the loyalist army, consisting entirely of infantry, was thrown forward in the direction of Centcotl, and kept up a fusillade, under cover of which the cavalry in scattered groups tried to cross. The insurgents, however, could not be dislodged from the opposite bank, and it was impossible to accomplish the passage under their persistent musketry. For close on three miles along the banks of the river this line of sharp-shooters extended, and at each end of the line artillery thundered incessantly. Men on either side were dropping every moment, and it seemed as though each army would annihilate the other without either crossing the stream. For four hours the battle had been raging without the combatants coming to close quarters, and Xuarez's soldiers remaining ever on the defensive, began to grow impatient. On the other hand, the Royalists trying to carry the passage of the stream by dash after dash, were warming up to their work.

It would have been madness for Don Hypolito to cross the stream, and with his few attack the many of the loyalists. The river was his great safeguard, and so long as that interposed its waters between him and the enemy, he felt comparatively safe, trusting to hold his position until the arrival of the Indians from the north, whom he counted upon taking the enemy in the rear. He saw plainly that his men were growing weary of remaining solely on the defensive, and submitting to be cut to pieces by the fire of Benito's artillery; but, until he saw a prospect of being reinforced by the Indians, he was powerless to do anyanything but stubbornly prevent the loyalists from fording the stream.

General Benito saw that the rebel leader was unaware of the disaffection of the allies, and relied on their arriving shortly to turn the tide of war in his favour. With a view, therefore, to dishearten him, he ordered an Indian scout, attached to his staff, to ford the river if possible, below the battery point, present himself to Xuarez as a deserter from the loyalists, and inform him that the Indians had retreated. The scout at once obeyed, and attempted to swim the river, but just as he was close on the opposite bank, a rifle-shot struck him, and it was with the greatest difficulty that he regained the shore. Several rebel soldiers ran up to finish him with their bayonets, but he implored them to take him to Xuarez, as he was in possession of certain facts relating to the allies.

On being brought into the presence of the rebel leader, he had just time to tell Don Hypolito of the uselessness of counting on the Indians, and shortly afterwards expired. Xuarez thought at first it was a device of the loyalists to gain time, but as hour after hour went on, and no Indians appeared, he began to believe that he was indeed foolish to depend upon help from that quarter. The full terror of his position came on him at once. He saw that, deserted by the Indians, cut off from Acauhtzin, the whole success of the rebellion against the Junta depended upon his cutting the army of Benito to pieces. Janjalla was behind him, and he several times thought of falling back on that town, but the knowledge that it was being bombarded by the loyalist fleet withheld him from committing such a folly. Centcotl was held in the interests of the Junta. There was no chance of safety there, so he saw that he must remain in his present position, and either tire out Benito by holding his position stubbornly, or dash across the river with the main portion of his troops, and try the fortune of war in a hand-to-hand fight.

With characteristic boldness he decided on the latter of these alternatives, and sent forward a thousand cavalry to cross the river, and carry the war into the enemy's camp. Midway between the two batteries, which still kept up their fire, he brought fifteen field-guns to bear on the masses of infantry on the other bank, armed only with their rifles, hoping to cut them to pieces, and thus afford his cavalry a safe landing. Benito ordered five gatling guns to silence the field battery, and prevent, if possible, the landing of the insurgent cavalry. Unfortunately, his orders could not be accomplished smartly enough, and before the gatlings could be brought into position, the field-guns of Xuarez had opened a heavy fire on the infantry, under cover of which five hundred horsemen crossed the stream. The landing once effected, others followed, and the cavalry rode down the infantry like sheep, while right and left the balls from the field-guns of Xuarez cut passages in the crowded masses. For the moment the advantage was decidedly with Don Hypolito.

At once a thousand cavalry, held in reserve behind the battery, were hurled forward on the horsemen of the rebels. Five hundred had now crossed the stream, and there held the loyalists at bay while their comrades formed. The rebel regiment pierced like a wedge into the mass of infantry, and met the cavalry of Benito some distance from the bank of the river. What with these horsemen, and the incessant firing of the field-guns, the infantry of Benito were thoroughly demoralised, and flying in all directions. The cavalry of Xuarez, with admirable discipline, formed into lines as soon as they crossed the river, and steadily drove the horsemen of the loyalists backward.

Xuarez at once took advantage of this gain, and, behind his cavalry, sent regiment after regiment of infantry with orders to carry the battery of Benito by storm. In vain the foot-soldiers of the loyalists were hurled against the advancing mass of rebel horse and foot now marching steadily for the battery. They did not give way one inch. Xuarez hoped to capture the battery, turn the guns against the loyalists, and then bringing the rest of his troops across the stream.

This unexpected manœuvre had taken Benito by surprise, and there was but little doubt that if the battery were captured a panic would ensue amongst his own men, and thus give Xuarez a decided advantage. The columns of rebels pouring across the stream pierced the host of loyalists like a wedge and bore steadily down on the battery which was still under the heavy fire of the insurgent artillery posted on the sandhills.

Things looked black at that moment for the loyalist army, but at this critical juncture the troops of Benito succeeded in forcing the passage of the stream further up near the city. What the Opposidores had done in the centre of the line they did at its end, and, under cover of a heavy fire from their gatlings, managed to cross the stream and capture the field-guns of the enemy. These were at once utilised and turned on the rebels, and in a few minutes were pouring a deadly fire into the masses of cavalry and infantry sent to hold the bridge passage by Xuarez. An officer galloped post-haste to Benito, informing him of the crossing of the stream, and the General recognising that he might cut off the forces of Xuarez on the left bank, sent to the bridge all the soldiers he could spare, amounting to some fifteen hundred.

Meanwhile the cavalry of Xuarez, supported by several regiments of infantry, were trying to carry the battery of the loyalists by storm. Their own artillery was now silent, as so inextricably mingled were rebels and loyalists round the battery that it was impossible for the gunners of Xuarez to fire without cutting their own men to pieces. The rebels were still steadily pouring, column after column, across the stream in the rear of the cavalry, when suddenly their line was cut in two by the victorious loyalists from the bridge.

These had utterly beaten the rebels defending the passage, by turning their own guns on them, and now those latter were flying towards the centre of the scene of operations, followed by a scattered body of cavalry, cutting them down in all directions. The loyalist infantry quickly crossed the river, and followed in the rear of the horsemen, but, being on foot, were necessarily far behind. The rebels attempted to re-form and reach the point where their columns were fording the stream but, flushed with victory, the cavalry of Benito passed clean through the mass, cutting off all further rebels from joining their comrades on the opposite shore.

At the same time, owing to the deadly fire of the loyalist battery, the invading soldiers of Xuarez were beginning to give way, and slowly fell back inch by inch towards the point where they had crossed. They were unable to get back, however, as the cavalry of Benito held them in check on the opposite bank, and seeing this, the General threw forward two regiments across the stream further up, where the bank, owing to the clean sweep made by his cavalry, was undefended.

The rebels now found themselves between two masses of their foes, between two fires, with nothing

but the river between.   They slowly retreated before
the infantry, pressing forward from the direction of
the battery, and falling back on the right bank of
the river, found themselves unable to cross in the
teeth of the loyalist cavalry holding the opposite
bank, while the foot-soldiers behind fought viciously
with the rebels.   The cavalry and infantry of Xuarez
thus caught became demoralized, and unable to keep
a firm front to the loyalists, broke up into terrified
masses, which were either cut to pieces, or forced into
the stream, where they were shot down by their
enemies on the opposite bank.

It was now close on six o'clock, and, after five
hours' incessant fighting, the advantage was now with
the army of the Junta. Benito held the passage of the
bridge near Centeotl, and from thence down to the
battery, the banks of the stream on both sides were
held by his own men.   The enemy beaten on the right
bank, were slowly falling back on the left, and concentrating themselves round the hillocks, from which
thundered their artillery.   Behind the battery, Xuarez
still held three thousand men in reserve, and these he
brought forward, with the intention of hurling them

in one last effort of despair, against the advancing masses of the loyalists.

General Benito no longer held back his army, but in person led his soldiers across the river. In a miraculously short space of time the combat was transferred from the right to the left bank of the Rio Tardo, and the whole force of the loyalists, with the exception of the corps of engineers attending to the battery, had crossed the river, and were pressing forward to carry the citadel of Xuarez by storm.

What with killed and wounded, and prisoners taken, the number of fighting men on either side was terribly reduced ; yet, numerically speaking, the advantage lay with the loyalists, who could oppose seven thousand men to four thousand on the part of Xuarez. Confident in his position, and in the shelter afforded by the sandhills, Don Hypolito gathered his four thousand round the base of his batteries, and played his guns with deadly effect on the advancing masses of the loyalists over the heads of his own men. It was now a hand-to-hand struggle, and though the loyalists had the advantage over the rebels in numbers, yet as they were unable to bring

their guns across the river, the combat was more or
less equalised. The deadly fire from the sandhills
played havoc with their ranks, and they were mowed
down in hundreds. Having no artillery to oppose
these guns, and being unable to silence them by the
battery on the opposite bank, the only hope of
thrashing the enemy lay in carrying the sandhills by
storm. This Benito, with desperate courage, now
proceeded to do.

As yet, Xuarez had managed to keep the loyalists
in front, and gathering his lines from the river bank
to some distance into the plain, desperately resisted
the attempts of the attacking force to break through
and storm the battery. To protect his rear from the
river side, he sent two hundred cavalry to the back of
the sandhills, to guard the stream lest any straggling
parties of loyalists should cross at that point and
assail him unexpectedly. He was now entirely on
the defensive, and, unless he succeeded in putting the
loyalists to flight with his artillery, saw not how he
could hope to win the victory.

How bitterly did he regret the desertion of the
Indians, the cause of which disaffection he could not

understand. With them coming from the north, he might have effected a conjunction by crossing the river as he had done, and thus captured the battery of Benito. As it was, however, his soldiers had been beaten back, the loyalists had crossed the river, and now his whole force was concentrated round the sandhills, upon which was placed his artillery.

In his despair, Don Hypolito longed for the darkness, in the hope that under cover of the night he might be enabled to fall back on Janjalla. Long since he would have done this but for the timely information that the town was blockaded by the warships of the Junta. It seemed like madness to retreat into such a death-trap, and yet if it could hold out against the bombardment until he arrived, he would at least have walls behind which to fight. He regretted intensely that he had not captured Centeotl and thrown himself therein to defend himself against the loyalists. Surrounded by stone walls, he could hope to wear out the troops of the Republic, and perhaps destroy them in detachments, but as it was he had no shelter. His whole front was being assaulted by the loyalists, and behind he had but his battery and a possible chance of falling back on Janjalla in the night-time.

The whole plain from Centeotl to the point of action was now in the hands of the loyalists, and seeing this the Jefe Politico of the city threw open the gates and sent forward men with provisions and wine to the wearied troops. Three hundred soldiers yet remained within the walls, and these also marched out to join the army of the Republic, and attack Xuarez in his last position. It was now past seven o'clock, and the darkness was rapidly coming on. Don Hypolito hoped that the loyalists would withdraw and renew the combat next day. In the interval, his men could rest and sustain themselves with food or fall back at once on Janjalla.

This respite, however, Benito declined to give. While the light lasted, he determined to keep up the fight, and if possible dislodge Xuarez from his position before the morning. Deeply did he regret that he had no electric lights, by the glare of which to conduct the battle; but as it was he took advantage of the clear twilight, and pushed forward his men vigorously in attempting to break down the stubborn line of defence offered by Don Hypolito.

It is questionable how long this state of things would have lasted, as the rebels obstinately fought on, and though Benito hurled column after column against them, not one inch would they yield. The artillery also, from the heights above, was sweeping down his rearward troops. He sent one thousand across the river again, to attempt the rear of the enemy, under cover of the fire of fifteen gatlings, but Xuarez turned four heavy guns on the passage of the river, and stopped the crossing with ease.

"Carrajo!" muttered Benito, shutting up his glass in a rage, "they will hold out till it is dark, and then we must stop. During the night they will fall back on Janjalla."

"And into the hands of our men!" replied Jack, who was standing beside the general. "No, Señor, Don Hypolito knows it is worse than useless to retreat from his present position. When the morning dawns, you will find him still on those hills."

"Bueno! All the same, Don Juan, I would like to finish him off to-night."

L 2

" Then send scouts from Centeotl to see if our men are advancing from Janjalla."

" It might be that the city is not taken."

" That is true. On the other hand, it might be that the city is."

Coincidences occur in real life as well as in novels and here occurred a case in point. Tim, who had been to Centeotl to make inquiries, galloped up to Benito at this moment and saluted.

" General," he said rapidly, " messengers have just arrived from Janjalla. The city is in the hands of the Junta, and our troops, to the number of two thousand, are pushing forward by forced marches."

" Janjalla in our hands?" cried Benito, joyfully. " Then Xuarez has no refuge on which to fall back."

The army shouted on hearing this cheering news, and looked upon the destruction of the rebels as a foregone conclusion, as indeed it was. Xuarez heard the shouting, and, becoming aware of the cause by the frequent cries of " Janjalla," ground his teeth with rage, as he saw how fortune was against him.

" Señores," he said to his officers, " we are condemned to stay here. There is now no hope of falling back on the seaport. We can but face the enemy, and fight bravely. I should have heard of this fall before, as my scouts are all over the country to Janjalla."

Nevertheless, in spite of this discouraging news, he urged his men to fight bravely, hoping that the night would come, and force the loyalists to withdraw for some hours. In that time his army could rest and eat, while he himself might think of some plan by which to circumvent the tactics of General Benito. He was quite ignorant that two thousand men were marching from Janjalla to attack him in the rear.

The last glimmer of the sunset had long since died out of the sky, and it was now comparatively dark. As yet, the reinforcements from Janjalla had not arrived and Benito was almost on the point of ceasing the fight till dawn, when the moon arose in the west. Her appearance was welcomed by him with joy, for her light was quite brilliant enough to enable the assaulting party to continue fighting ; and incessantly pressing on the wearied troops of Xuarez seemed the only chance of beating him from the sandhills and scattering his army. Don Hypolito cursed the moon audibly, for he saw that his last chance of escaping in the darkness was gone. Nothing remained for him but to fight on doggedly.

Then his scouts arrived, and he learned that in an hour two thousand men would attack him in the rear. With a cry of rage, he hurled his field-glass down the hill.

"Fortune is against me," he muttered, biting his lip with wrath ; "my star goes down in blood. Attacked front and rear, I cannot hold out much longer."

Yet he was too brave to give in, and, seeing that the town of Centeotl was left defenceless, as its garrison had joined Benito, he hoped to make a detour, and throw himself with his remaining troops into the city. One thousand men he could leave to defend the battery and draw off the attention of the loyalists, and with his remaining two thousand march silently away to the south, then make a detour for the city. Then the reinforcements would come up in vain, for he and his men would have slipped away like an eel from between the two armies. He never thought of the fate of the thousand men he was leaving behind. But at that moment he would have given anything to gain time to reconstruct his plans, and would have sacrificed a million lives so that his campaign should not end in disaster.

This mad scheme to occupy Centeotl in the teeth of the enemy was destined to fail for lack of time. Before he could move a single column towards the city, the sound of distant firing was heard, and the reinforcements came up in the rear at a quick trot. The whole force of Xuarez was disposed along the front of the battery, protecting it from the assaults of Benito's army. Undefended in the rear, save for two hundred cavalry guarding the river, it offered itself freely to the reinforcements for storming. Don Hypolito brought round troops rapidly from the front to oppose this new danger. The cavalry dashed recklessly between the battery and the advancing infantry from Janjalla. Three guns, with depressed muzzles, rained down shot on the masses of infantry. It was all in vain. The fresh troops, elated by the fall of Janjalla, and the crossing of the river by General Benito, passed clean over the thin line of cavalry drawn up to beat them back. A mass of men obliterating man and horse, rolled upward towards the hastily formed lines of weary soldiers, brought round from the front to protect the rear. These succumbed in a few minutes, and the guns no longer being able to do damage by reason of the enemy being directly under their muzzles, the reinforcements swarmed up the slanting slope of the sandhills with cries of victory.

Benito heard those cries, and at once guessed that the troops from Janjalla were carrying the battery by storm. Hitherto he had been holding five hundred cavalry and two thousand infantry in reserve. These were now brought forward and hurled on the soldiers of Xuarez massed at the foot of the sandhills. The rebels looked in front, and saw this mass threatening to overwhelm them; they looked behind, and lo! over the brow of the sandhills poured a black crowd of men over whose heads floated the yellow standard of the Republic. The guns were silenced, the gunners bayoneted, and the red flag of Xuarez dragged from its pole at the top of the hill. Xuarez himself, surrounded by a ring of his officers, waved his sword for a moment, and then the wave of men passed over him. A cry spread throughout the host of rebels that he was lost. The men at the base of the sandhills,

seeing the wave of men rolling downward, lost heart
and broke up into scattered masses. On came the
army of Benito, and between the two forces the
insurgents crumpled up like paper.

In all directions they fled like sheep, and were
chased for miles by the victorious Republicans.
Benito, a merciful man, strove to restrain the zeal of
his soldiers. It was all in vain, they were drunken
with victory, and sabred and shot the wretched
fugitives without mercy. The smoke hung heavily
over the field of battle, and when it cleared away, the
victorious troops of the Junta saw the great standard
of the Republic floating proudly in the place lately
occupied by the battery of the enemy.

Don Hypolito had disappeared, his army, broken
to pieces, was flying in all directions. From the
triumphant army massed round the sandhills, rose a
roar of joy which made the earth tremble. The wind
which had blown away the smoke, shook out the
folds of the opal flag, and the Cholacacians saluted
the invincible banner with cheers.

"Viva el opale! Viva el Republica!"

CHAPTER IX.

THE TRIUMPH OF THE REPUBLIC.

Mars, god of war,
Whom we abhor,
Hath doffed his helm,
And laid his lance and shield aside.
He will no more
Lay waste our store,
Nor overwhelm
Our lands beneath his crimson tide.

Peace comes anon,
Now war hath gone,
Her olive bough
Of gentleness and quiet she brings
Beneath her sway,
No deadly fray
Can fright us now;
From battle plains the harvest springs.

THREE weeks after that memorable victory at Centeotl, the city of Tlatonac was holding high festival in honour of the triumphant Junta. Every · street was illuminated and decorated with flowers. In the principal places, fireworks, so dear to the hearts of the Cholacacans were being let off, and the ships lying in the harbour were brilliant with lights. The populace in their gayest attire walked singing through the streets, visited the pulque shops, and gathered in groups to indulge in their national dances. Bands stationed in different squares, played the Opal Fandango, The March of Zuloaga, and soldiers, the heroes of the hour, were to be seen everywhere, being fêted and caressed by the grateful citizens.

Before the Palacio Nacional a dense crowd had collected, and the place itself, brilliantly lighted up, was occupied by a gaily dressed throng. His Excellency the President was giving a ball in honour of the establishment of peace. On one of the balconies Jack and Dolores were seated, watching the varied throng below, and talking of past events. For the hundredth time Dolores was asking Jack about the battle, and all that had taken place thereat.

" I am sure, Dolores, you must be wearied of this more than twice-told tale."

" No, Juanito! It is a tale of which I never weary. Come, querido, tell me once more. Begin, ' After the battle——' "

"After the battle," repeated Jack, humouring her fancy. "Well, the first thing we did after the battle was to search for the body of Don Xuarez. He had been last seen on the summit of the sandhill by his battery. When the reinforcements took that position by storm, Xuarez vanished, and though we searched everywhere for his body, it could not be found."

"So then you knew that he had escaped?"

"It was presumed so; but even now we are not certain as to what has become of him. However, he had vanished; and giving up the search for him, dead or alive, in despair, General Benito left a few hundred men to garrison Centeotl, and pushed on at once to Janjalla. In the harbour we found the fleet, which had captured the town by bombarding it, and Captain Pedraza, under instructions from Benito, took the ships back to Tlatonac."

"Ah, I remember how joyful we were when they entered the harbour and announced the victory. Everyone in Tlatonac was mad with joy."

"Dios! They are mad enough to-night," said Jack, smiling, as he looked down on the crowd; "but under the circumstances, I think it is excusable. The fall of Acauhtzin, the last stronghold of the Opposidores, is worth being excited about. Did Rafael tell you all about it, Dolores?"

"Not so much as he might have done," pouted Dolores, unfurling her fan; "but you see, Juan, there is Doña Carmencita——"

"Of course! Poor girl! Fancy her father being killed when the city was being bombarded!"

"A great loss, was it not?" sighed Dolores, her eyes filling with tears. "Ay di mi. How sad would I feel had I lost my dear uncle."

"It is the fortune of war," said Jack, calmly. "Instead of our troops capturing Acauhtzin and killing Tejada, it might have been Xuarez storming Tlatonac and shooting Don Miguel. One thing, at least, Doña Carmencita has to be grateful for: Rafael rescued her unharmed from the burning city, and now she is to be his wife."

"And I am to be yours!"

"Yes; and Eulalia is to be Philip's," finished Jack, promptly. "I thought Don Miguel would never give his consent to that marriage."

"Eh, Juanito!" said Dolores, with a mischievous

smile, "I think my uncle did so to console Don Felipe for losing his chance of being at the battle."

"Poor Philip! Only one battle of any consequence, and he missed it by being away at Truxillo."

At this moment Dolores was summoned away from her lover by Doña Serafina. The old lady was a very severe duenna when not asleep, and as Dolores was yet unmarried, did not approve of her being too much in the society of her future husband. A little jealousy was mingled with this strict regard for etiquette, as Doña Serafina had utterly failed to fascinate Peter. All her smiles and insinuating remarks had been quite thrown away on the little doctor, who showed no disposition for matrimony, and scrupulously ignored the languishing looks of his elderly admirer. Finally, Serafina gave up the pursuit of this medical male as a bad job, and revenged herself indirectly on the sex by being particularly sharp with Eulalia and Dolores, both of whom were rarely permitted to be more than a few minutes with their respective lovers. These last blamed Peter in no measured terms for thus depriving them of the society of their future wives ; but the doctor absolutely refused to sacrifice himself any longer on the altar of friendship. He announced this in a conversation which took place in the patio of Casa Maraquando after the ball.

" I would do anything for you I could," he explained plaintively to.Jack and Philip ; "but I really cannot go on paying attention to Doña Serafina. She thinks I am in earnest ! "

" And so you ought to be, you little monster," said Tim, quickly. " It's time you were married."

" Well, then, why don't you set the example ? "

" It's easy talking ! I have no one to love me."

" Journalism is a jealous mistress," observed Philip, laughing. " Tim is devoted to ' Articles from a Special Correspondent.' "

" True for you," replied Tim, complacently ; " but my occupation's gone. Didn't I send my last article about ' The Fall of Acauhtzin ' from Janjalla ? and isn't the war over ? "

" The war is certainly over ! " said Jack, lighting a cigarette; " but the danger of another war is not yet past."

" What do you mean, Jack ? "

"Don Hypolito still lives ; and while he lives, the Republic is not safe."

"Still lives !" echoed Philip, in surprise. "Why, Jack, I don't see how you can make that out. He was not found on the field of battle, nor in Janjalla, nor in Acauhtzin. He must be dead ! "

"No ; Don Hypolito is not the man to die so easily. Where he is, I do not know, but I am certain he is yet alive."

There was silence for a few minutes, as each was busy with his own thoughts regarding the probable resurrection of Xuarez. After the battle of Centeotl, he had vanished utterly from the face of the earth. It was thought he had fled to Janjalla, or perchance to Acauhtzin ; but in neither of those towns could he be discovered. After a bombardment of five hours, the latter city had surrendered to the warships. Don José, the Governor, in the absence of Xuarez, had been killed by the bursting of a bomb, and many of his officers had shared the same fate. Of Xuarez, however, nothing could be discovered, and Don Miguel was much disturbed thereat. With a restless spirit like the rebel leader still working in secret, the danger was not yet at an end, and the President was determined to spare no effort to bring Xuarez, to justice. While the four friends were thinking over this matter, Don Rafael, who had been holding a private conversation with his father, entered the patio.

That young man was the hero of the bombardment of Acauhtzin. He had recovered Doña Carmencita; his father had consented to his speedy marriage with that lady, and he was idolised by his fellow-citizens. With all this good fortune, he should have been gay and lighthearted; but as he entered the patio, he certainly looked anything but happy.

"Dios! What ails you, Rafael?" asked Jack, as his friend threw himself into a seat, and sighed heavily. "Anything wrong?"

"Carambo! Everything is wrong. My father refuses his consent to our marriages."

"What?" interrupted Philip and Jack, in dismay.

"Till Xuarez is discovered and punished," finished Rafael, dismally.

"Ah!" said Philip, with a breath of relief, "it might have been worse. I thought you were about

to say Don Miguel had refused his consent altogether."

" Dios !   I don't know if it does not amount to
that," replied Rafael, shrugging his shoulders. " How
are we to find this ladron of a Xuarez?   He is not
at Acauhtzin.   He is not in the south.   Where then
are we to look for him ?"

" Can you not find out? —— "

" I can find out nothing, mi amigo.   For my part,
I believe he is dead."

" For my part, Señor Rafael, I believe he is alive,"
retorted Tim, gruffly.

" Eh !   And where do you think he is to be found,
Señor Corresponsal ? "

"Quien sabe," said Tim, carelessly. "But you know,
Señor, that after the battle of Centeotl, I rode to Janjalla, to wire my report to England ? "

" Yes."

" While there, I heard two prisoners talking. They,
deeming me to be a foreigner, and not knowing
that I was conversant with Spanish, spoke freely."

" Bueno !   And they said ? —— "

" Nothing about Don Hypolito, but talked of Pepe."

"Pepe!" echoed Philip, quickly. "The zambo who decoyed Dolores from Tlatonac—the lover of Marina?"

"The same. Pepe, it appears, had followed Xuarez to Janjalla, being, as we know, the prince of spies. When *The Cortes* was taken, and Xuarez was thus cut off from getting back to Acauhtzin, Pepe happened to be in Janjalla. The troops of Xuarez were wondering, in the case of defeat, how they could escape from the hands of our men. Pepe laughed, on hearing their doubts, and said he could easily escape to Totatzine."

"To Totatzine?"

"To the sacred city. He said no one could follow him there, and that he knew of a secret way in the south, which would take him thither."

"But, Jack, the secret way you came is to the north of Tlatonac," said Philip turning towards Duval.

"Very true! But for a long time I have had my suspicions that there is a second way to that city, by the cañon road, of which I told you. It is by that way, to my mind, that Pepe intended to go."

"Yes, mi amigo!" said Rafael, triumphantly; "but

M 2

you quite forget. Pepe was captured in the south, after the battle of Centeotl, and is now in prison at Tlatonac, awaiting punishment."

"Very true! He did not escape to Totatzine, as he intended. But where was he captured? At the battle of Centeotl. Now, seeing that Don Hypolito has disappeared, it is just possible that Pepe told him of the second secret way to the sacred city, and that Xuarez may have escaped thence."

"Dios!" exclaimed Rafael, springing to his feet. "Think you, Señor Corresponsal, that this dog is now at Totatzine?"

"I am not sure, but it might be so. Ixtlilxochitli is his friend. There he would be safe, and if at the battle of Centeotl Pepe told him of this southern way to the city, when he saw that all was lost, he probably took advantage of the information."

"Why not find out if this is so, from Pepe?" suggested Jack, when Tim ceased speaking.

"He will tell nothing," replied Rafael, in disgust. "This zambo is a mule for obstinacy."

"We might try, at all events," said Philip, cheerfully. "Where is Pepe, mi amigo?"

" In the prison of the Palacio Nacional.   If you think, Señores, there is any chance of getting information from the zambo, let us seek him now."

" Why to-night ? " said Peter, looking at his watch, " or rather this morning.   It is two o'clock.   You are all weary with the ball.   Better wait till to-morrow."

" No ! " exclaimed Rafael, throwing his heavy cloak over his shoulder.   " We will go now.   My father absolutely refuses to let any of us marry until we discover Xuarez.   I want to know where he is to be found at once, otherwise I shall get no rest.   As for you, señor——"

" I will come, by all means," said Philip, putting on his sombrero.   " It is also to my interest to find Xuarez, else I may not marry your sister, Rafael."

" We will all go ! " said Jack, rising to his feet. " Tim, you may get some copy, and make an article of it—' The Confessions of a Spy.'   Peter, you can go to bed, as this matter does not interest you in the least."

" Oh, doesn't it ? " said Peter, indignantly.   " I am as anxious as you are to see you married, Jack.   But with your permission, I shall go to bed, because I do not think you'll get any information out of Pepe."

"We'll try, at all events," observed, Philip, emphatically. "I want to marry Eulalia."

"And I," said Juan, following his friends to the door, "want to do three things, none of which I can accomplish unless Pepe tells us of the secret way."

"And the three things, Jack?" asked Tim, curiously.

"First, I want to marry Dolores. Second, I desire to save the life of Cocom, who is a prisoner at Totatzine ; and, third, I am anxious to obtain possession again of the harlequin opal."

CHAPTER X.

THE CAÑON ROAD.

This is a tropical forest,
Where myriad leaves forming a roof overhead, keep out the efful-
    gence of sunlight,
So that beneath is the region of shadows and dimness ;
Yet in this spectral twilight rise cities, magnificent, lonely ;
Built in the far-distant days of giants—great architects they !
Sky-piercing pyramids, plinth, and column, and capital.
Line upon line of pillars, that loom in the darkness eternal,
Staircases huge, vast halls, and temples majestical ;
Now no longer receiving the throngs of worshippers holy,
Only the bat flits through the ruins; ravenous beasts now wander
Through street, and square, and palaces gorgeous.
Who built all these splendours ?   We know not who built them.
Yet do they loom in the twilight region of shadows,
Encircled by tropical forests.

As a rule, Dr. Grench was an early riser, and denied
himself the luxurious idleness of morning slumbers,
but on this special occasion he did not wake at his
usual hour.   The dancing of the previous night had
proved too much for the virtuous Peter, who always
went to bed early, consequently he was very tired, and

by no means pleased at being awakened unexpectedly by Jack. Peter was in the middle of a delightful dream, in which he was hunting unusually large beetles. After a time, however, the beetles began to hunt Peter, and one, having caught him, was shaking him severely. The shaking woke him up, and the beetle changed to Jack, who was trying to pull Peter out of bed.

"What's matter?" grumbled Peter vaguely, struggling into a sitting position. "I don't want to get up."

"You must," said Jack, serenely, "or we shall start without you."

"Start? what? where? when? Beetle-hunting?"

"Peter, you are not awake! What do you mean by such delirious talk? Put on your clothes, and come down to breakfast. We're all waiting."

Jack vanished, and Peter, wondering what was the matter, got out of bed with manifest reluctance. A cold bath drove the fumes of sleep from his head, and dressing rapidly, he repaired to the dining-room, where he found his friends and Rafael making a hasty meal. Peter stared, and began to ask questions.

"Now what is——?"

"Oh, here's Peter," said Philip, looking up with a smile. " Come on, sluggard, and have something to eat. We are going to Cuavaca by train."

"Train!" repeated the doctor, taking his seat. " What train ?"

"Jack's train, you idiot," said Tim, giving Peter a dig in the ribs. " Your wits are wandering!"

" I think yours must be," retorted Peter, addressing the company collectively. "What is the meaning of this early rising ?"

" We are going to Cuavaca."

" Never heard of it."

"Then you hear of it now," said Jack, crossly; "how stupid you are, Peter. I will explain : we saw Pepe, the zambo, last night, and on condition that his life is spared, he has promised to guide us to the city of Totatzine by this second secret way."

" Oh! and Cuavaca ?"

"Cuavaca is a town thirty miles inland. The railway line is laid down to that place, and twenty miles beyond. We are taking a thousand troops to Cuavaca, and intend to leave them there, while Pepe shows us the cañon road. Then we will lead them by that way to Totatzinc, save Cocom, take Xuarez prisoner, and secure the opal."

" But," said Peter, argumentatively, " is the end of your railway near this hidden city? or does a trackless forest lie between the terminus and the cañon road ?"

Jack made a diagram on the tablecloth with knives and plates.

" Look, Peter ! This is Tlatonac. This Cuavaca. We go to the latter place by rail. From Cuavaca the railway is constructed another twenty miles, and stops in the middle of a vast forest. Here, according to Pepe, is Totatzine, sunken out of sight in its hollow valley. Between the end of the railway and Totatzine is a distance of twenty miles, more or less —— "

" Of tangled forest and brushwood ! "

" Nothing of the sort. Don't I tell you Pepe has promised to show us the secret way—the other secret way? The entrance is from a ruined city, about a mile to the right of the railway works. We find out that city, take our men from Cuavaca to it, and thence march up the cañon road to Totatzine."

" Dios ! Don Juan ! " exclaimed Rafael, who had been looking at Jack's table-map. " It seems to me that if the railway goes on it will pass by and reveal this hidden city."

" Not it. Had there been a chance of its doing so, we would have had trouble with the Indians pulling up the rails. No, mi amigo. The line is surveyed a long distance further on. If it turned to the right, it might certainly hit Totatzine; but, as you see, it trends to the left, and if used for a century could never reveal the existence of the sacred city. Ixtlil-xochitli saw that, and did not mind the railway passing, so to speak, by his door. The city is too well hidden by its encircling mountains and by the windings of the cañon to be discovered without special exploration."

" But it seems to me awfully stupid that the priests should take so much trouble over the one secret way and never bother about the other."

This observation of Philip's seemed to strike Jack, and he reflected a few moments before he replied.

" What you say is very true, Philip," he replied slowly ; " the secret way leading to the sea is very complicated, and even then the priests always blind-fold pilgrims on the platform. This other road, leading from the ruined city, must be blocked up by rubbish, and what not. There is a wall across the entrance to the cañon, but it is pierced by a gate always open. No one comes by the narrow track, so I expect the entrance to that road has been choked up, and the way fallen into disuse."

"Then how did Pepe find it out?"

"Lord knows! But the secret must be his alone else the priests would have destroyed the cañon path leading to the pierced wall, and so cut off communication entirely from that side of the town."

"I hope Pepe is not leading us into an ambush," said Peter, anxiously, as they arose to go.

"If he does, it will cost him his life," replied Philip, grimly. "Pepe, my dear doctor, marches before us with a pistol at his head. The first signs of treachery, and he falls dead. I don't think he'll risk that catastrophe."

By this time Peter had concluded his breakfast, and they all set out to the Puerta de la Culebra, near which, beyond the walls, was the railway station. On the previous night Pepe, under promise of his life being spared, had admitted that Don Hypolito had fled northward overland to Totatzinc, gaining the city by the inland secret way. This road Pepe promised to reveal on condition that the President spared his life. Next morning, Rafael told his father of the offer, and, as Don Miguel was anxious to capture Xuarez, he readily assented to the proposition of the zambo.

Of course the six thousand Indians, who had been disbanded by the influence of the opal, were not in the sacred city. Their villages were far to the north, near Acauhtzin, and as they only came south to the festivals of the opal, by the secret way of the sea, it was unlikely that the troops led by Rafael and Jack would encounter any resistance. The forests where the railway ended, and where, according to Pepe, the cañon road began, were singularly devoid of population. This might have been caused by the jealousy of the priests, lest some wandering Indians should find the entrance to the cañon road from the ruined city. If so, this jealous suspicion caused their ruin ; for, had the district been infested with Indians, they, seeing an unusual concourse of soldiers at Cuavaca, would at once have warned the priests of the intended invasion of Totatzine. Then the cañon road could have been easily defended against the troops from Tlatonac by a small body of defenders, and the disaster averted. As it was, however, the inhabitants of the sacred city were entirely ignorant of their danger until the foe was under their walls.

The railway line was completed as far as Cuavaca, a little inland village which promised to shortly develop into a city, owing to its being the future starting place, whence lines were to run north and south throughout the whole length of Cholacaca. From the capital to this terminus extended a vast plain for over thirty miles, so that there was no difficulty in laying the line, and it had been speedily completed under the vigorous superintendence of Jack. There were no engineering difficulties to be overcome, and the railway ran easily in a straight line over the plains to the foot of the volcano Xicotencatl, where Cuavaca was situated. From this point began a rugged and mountainous country, which extended northward as far as Acauhtzin. Twenty miles of railway had been constructed with great difficulty, as, owing to the configuration of the country, the line was singularly curving and irregular. Bridges had to be built across cañons, tunnels had to be pierced through solid rock, and embankments, faced with stone walls, constructed where the ground fell away rapidly to moderately sized plains. The district was situated in the tierra templada, about ten thousand feet above sea level; but, the grade constantly ascending as the iron road went northward, it was calculated by Jack that the last portion of the way would run some short distance below the snow line of the tierra friá.

This expedition to capture Totatzine was not without its dangers. It was the season of festival and the sacred city would doubtless be filled with fanatical worshippers, who would fiercely resist the attempted seizure of their shrines. A thousand well-armed infantry were sent to Cuavaca by Don Miguel, and, leaving these quartered in the village, Jack, with his three friends and Rafael, guided by Pepe, went forward to search for the secret entrance. When this was found, they intended to return and take the troops by railway twenty miles, and thence lead them by the secret entrance up the cañon road. When this was done, a reinforcement of another thousand soldiers was to arrive at Cuavaca, and await instructions there, lest the first should fail to capture the city. The engines running on the line from Cuavaca were singularly powerful machines, strongly built, so as to ascend the gradient to the northward, and there were plenty of trucks in which troops could be taken to the end of the railway. Jack also had a few carriages shifted from the Cuavaca line to that running northward, so that the whole body of soldiers now stationed at the little town could be conveyed to the hoped-for entrance of the cañon road in a remarkably short space of time.

By noon all the troops were quartered at Cuavaca, and then Jack started by the northern line for the cañon road. He only took an engine with one carriage, so as to travel as rapidly as possible. At first he wanted to go forward himself with Pepe, but Philip would in no way consent to his doing this.

"You can't trust that zambo, Jack," he said, decisively; "he might take advantage of your being alone, and knock you on the head."

"Scarcely, when I am armed and he is not. If

only we two go, we can travel on the engine. If you all come, I must fix on a carriage."

"Well, that won't make much difference," retorted Philip, quickly. "We are all keen on the business, and want to see how matters turn out. Tim, Peter, Rafael, and myself are all coming with you, Jack; so hitch on a carriage to your engine right away."

This was accordingly done without further objection on the part of Duval, and they left Cuavaca about one o'clock, travelling rapidly so as to reach the terminus with as little delay as possible. According to Pepe, it would take some hours for them to discover the ruined city, and they did not expect to return before six o'clock. Then it would have to be decided whether they would take the troops on to the ruined city at once, or wait till the next day.

Cuavaca was situate at the base of the great volcano Xicotencatl, which reared its white peak high above the surrounding mountains. North and south stretched ranges from the central point with summits more or less covered with snow, and from Cuavaca began dense forests which clothed the slopes of these mighty hills. Leaving the village by the side towards the north, the engine with its solitary carriage ran through a moderately long tunnel piercing a high range of hills, which shot outward at right angles from the principal mountains. From thence it emerged on to a deep valley, and skirted the side of the hills in a winding track cut out of the solid rock. Jack was on board the engine with the driver, personally super-intending the journey, and his three friends with Rafael were admiring the view from the windows of the carriage. Pepe, guarded by two soldiers, was seated at the end of the carriage, and looked anything but cheerful under such surveillance.

The scenery was truly wonderful. Sliding along the side of the mountains, those in the carriage look-ing out, saw not the line on which they were running, but looked down eight or nine hundred feet into the depths below. Sometimes the line was built of solid masonry clamped with iron, and it was anything but pleasant to think how the train was clinging like a fly to the perpendicular sides of the giant hills. Below swirled rapid torrents raging over black rocks, or flowing in broad streams between flat mud-banks. The engine would proceed along a level for some

distance, then pant slowly up an ascending gradient ;
suddenly turning a sharp curve, she would shoot
breathlessly down a decline on to a long narrow
bridge thrown across a wide expanse of river bed intersected by thin streams, which at time of rain joined
their forces into one vast flood. Owing to the infinite
windings of the line, it was built on the narrow gauge
system, so as to permit the quick turning of curves,
and when the engine, leaning to one side, shot round
these turnings, the sensation was anything but
pleasant.

"It's a most wonderful line, so far as engineering
goes," said Philip, drawing back from the window with
a sudden qualm, as the carriage rocked dangerously ;
"but it is devilishly unpleasant. If we went over !"

"There wouldn't be much of us left," said Tim
grimly. "Begad, Philip, I've been in a mighty lot of
railway trains, but this line of Jack's beats Banagher,
and Banagher beats the devil."

"Santissima!" said Rafael, uneasily, "I trust, Señores
this devil of an engine will not fall over the cliff."

"I'd never travel on this line for pleasure," cried
Peter, who was seated on the opposite side to the

N 2

precipice for safety; "nor do I think it will be much patronised by people when opened."

"The sea for me," remarked Philip, thankfully; "anything but being boxed up in this place, with a chance of falling five or six thousand feet without hope of getting out of the carriage."

In truth the journey was singularly unpleasant in many places. Jack had constructed his line thoroughly well; but there was no denying that the sudden turns, the unexpected descents, the narrow bridges, and the frequent tunnels, were enough to shake the nerves of the strongest man. On all sides arose the snow-clad peaks, far below ran rivers,spread forests,gaped cañons and between heaven and earth crawled the train, holding on to the sides of mountains. The colours and lights sweeping over the scenery were exquisite, the landscape below, above, was grand and impressive, but the four men in the carriage felt somewhat nervous at this tremendous journey. In ordinary cases, they were brave enough, and prepared for any emergency; but boxed up in this carriage they felt helpless should an accident occur. As to Jack, he was used to such travelling, and looked at his work with great pride.

At length the engine shot from a deep and narrow cutting into the depths of a broad-spreading forest, clothing a deep valley. Through its centre ran a torrent, and the line skirted this to the left, through dense woodland, towards the high peaks of a mountain in the far distance. Midway in this valley the engine slowed down, and ultimately stopped. Philip, looking out of the window, saw a wide clearing, with upturned soil, fallen trees, and here and there huts erected. It was the terminus of the railway; and, thankful to have arrived in safety, they all jumped out on to the sward with alacrity.

Beyond this clearing appeared a track cut through the forest, trending in the direction of the distant peaks, but the line stopped at the beginning of this avenue. Scattered rails, piles of sleepers, the abrupt termination of the line, showed that it went no further. Between this point and the unknown city of Totatzine intervened a distance of twenty miles. The little party, with their guns and revolvers all in order, stood looking around them at the unfinished line. Pepe, guarded by the two soldiers, was sullen and watchful.

"And where is Totatzine?" said Rafael, staring round this wilderness of trees.

Pepe pointed to the north-east, beyond the peaks.

"It is there, Señor.   In the hollow of the hills."

"And the buried city?"

"Bueno! I will show it to you, Señores."

"One moment, Pepe," said Jack, staying the zambo, as he turned off to the left, "how can you tell the way to this city from here?"

"Dios! Señor Americano, I escaped from Totatzine to this place four months ago. I was sent by Don Hypolito before the war to the priest Ixtlilxochitli, and he detained me in the city. I could not find the secret way to the sea, and one night went out through the wall on to the cañon road.   It led me many miles along the side of the cliffs, then down a staircase into a forest; at length, Señores, it took me through a tunnel. I had to climb over some rubbish of stones and earth up another staircase, and found myself in a large city of ruins. Leaving that, I pushed through the forest to the left, and came upon this clearing, where I found the men of the Señor Americano at work. They took me to Tlatonac, and there I remained till I went to Acauhtzin with Marina, as the Señor knows."

"Did you tell my men of your discovery of this way?" asked Jack, abruptly.

"No, Señor Americano. I feared the vengeance of the priests."

"Was the railway at this point four months ago, Jack?" asked Philip, looking round at the clearing.

"Yes. There was a possibility of war, and I was just going to England to get you to come here. The works were left in the condition you now see them. If this zambo escaped, as he says, he could easily have reached Tlatonac from this point."

"Bueno!" said Rafael, in a satisfied tone, "thus far his story is true. Let us go forward, amigos."

Jack made a sign to Pepe, who at once proceeded to walk towards the woods on the left, guarded by the two soldiers. His escort was well armed, so the zambo did not try to escape, knowing that before he could run a few yards he would have a bullet in his skull. The rest of the party followed, keeping their revolvers handy, in case of a possible surprise from Indians. They saw none, however, as the forest was completely deserted by all humanity. Pepe pushed forward through the brushwood, and they followed. In case they should lose their way, they blazed the trees with the hatchets with which they had taken care to provide themselves. Jack was resolved not to trust the zambo too far.

For about a mile they proceeded through a comparatively well-defined track in a north-western direction, then suddenly turned so as to face the distant peaks some fifteen miles away. This new path gradually broadened out into a wide avenue, and at the end of three miles, buildings, and ruins of walls began to make their appearance in a scattered fashion. At length, at the conclusion of another mile, they entered a paved road, adorned on either side by statues of Aztec deities, similar to those on the platform facing the sea.

" I cannot believe that this city is unknown," said Jack to Philip, as they marched on abreast behind Pepe and his guards.

" Why not? No one would suspect its existence from the railway clearing."

"No, that is true! But occasionally there must be some tribes of Indians about here, and they would be sure to hit upon it. Between the clearing and the beginning of this broad road it is but four miles, and the tracks seemed pretty well defined—clear enough at all events, to guide anyone hither. Once in this avenue, and it is easy to strike the city—as now."

They had emerged suddenly into a vast space, built over with mansions, palaces, temples, and mighty walls. A pyramid of earth, surmounted by a ruined teocalli, was placed in the centre of the city and the wide streets shot off from this omphalos in a similar way to those of Totatzine. In fact, on exploring the city thoroughly, Jack came to the conclusion that those who had built Totatzine had also constructed this place. The plan was precisely the same, and, judging from the massive buildings, the carven façades of the walls, the broad terraces, and the enormous flights of steps, it must have been a populous place of some importance.

"Judging from what we see, I think it must be a royal city," said Philip, looking awestruck at these colossal works of the dead. "Here, perchance, the king had his seat, and the secret way was constructed from this place to the sacred city of Totatzine, where the god Huitzilopochtli had his shrine."

"At all events, I have no doubt that this city is well known to the Indians of the present day," replied Jack, decisively; "though doubtless the entrance to the cañon road, choked up by rubbish, has escaped their notice. Did they know of its existence, Ixtlilxo-chitli would have closed up the narrow track leading round the precipice into the interior wall."

It was now between four and five o'clock, so they had not much time to lose if they desired to find the entrance before sunset. The engine, in charge of the driver, had been left in the clearing, Jack judging it would be quite safe there, as no Indians seemed to be in the vicinity. They had brought provisions with them, and if it was necessary, could camp out in the clearing till dawn, when they could go back to Cuavaca to bring the troops.

Pepe marched forward into the central square, and then led them towards the extreme end of the city. Here a surprise awaited them, for they found that the town was built against a vast cliff, some eighty or ninety feet in height. A lengthy temple, reached by a flight of steps, was cut out of the solid rock, with ranges of pillars massive in the design and architecture.

"Wonderful!" cried Philip, in amazement, as he surveyed the Cyclopean ruins; "these temples are like those of Petra. What great men must they have been who built such shrines! A great civilisation once flourished here, Jack."

"Without doubt," said Tim, who was much impressed by these grand remains; "these Toltecs, or whatever you call them, were greater than the Aztecs. Cortes, to my mind, found a vastly inferior civilisation than had been when these cities were built."

"Carajo, Señor Corresponsal!" cried Rafael, overhearing his remarks; "we have nothing like this in Tlatonac."

"Nor are likely to have," said Peter, dryly; "the Toltecs were greater builders than the Spaniards."

Guided by Pepe, they entered into this rock-hewn temple, and found themselves in a vast hall. At the back of the shrine, now unoccupied by any idol, appeared a ruined archway choked up with rubbish.

The explorers had taken the precaution of bringing torches with them, knowing there was a tunnel to be gone through. From this entrance, as Pepe informed them, it was fifteen miles to the hidden city of Totatzine. Lighting the torches, they climbed over the rubbish and fallen stones heaped in front of the archway, and began to ascend an immense staircase. Jack and Philip went first of all, followed by Pepe and his guards, after whom came the three remaining members of the party.

Up this staircase they ascended, and, at length emerging into the light of day, found themselves on a vast plateau, thickly covered with forests. A well-paved road, still gently ascending, stretched through these woods into the infinite distance. It was over-grown with brushwood and giant trees; still they found no difficulty in getting along, owing to the admirable way in which the stone blocks had been laid. This road ran for five miles, and then suddenly disappeared down a shallow flight of steps, under a low archway. Here Pepe stopped, and pointed down-ward.

"These steps, Señor Americano," he said, addressing

Jack, "lead down for a quarter of a mile, then along a tunnel for three-quarters of a mile. It brings you out on to the bed of the torrent flowing through the cañon. The narrow path leads from its mouth for nine miles to the pierced wall. When there, you are just below the walls of Totatzine."

Jack and his friends held a consultation as to the wisdom of proceeding further that night. The darkness was coming on, and it would be as well to get back to the clearing before the night. There they could camp out, and return to Cuavaca for the troops at dawn.

"For my part," said Philip, quietly, "I do not think we need explore further on our own account. Pepe has spoken truly up to the present, and without doubt this tunnel leads to the torrent of the cañon and the narrow path, as he describes. Let us return to the clearing, go back to Cuavaca, and bring on the troops. They can camp in the ruined city to-morrow night, and next morning can march to Totatzine."

The rest of the party agreed to this plan, and, leaving the shallow tunnel at the foot of the protecting range of the Totatzine mountains, they returned to the camp. Now that he had shown them the way, Pepe wanted to be set free; but this the whole party unanimously refused to do.

"No, no, my friend," said Rafael, making himself the mouthpiece of the others, "you may warn the Indians we are coming. Till Totatzine be taken by our troops, you are a prisoner."

Pepe was forced to abide by this decision, and composed himself to sleep in the clearing, watched vigilantly by his guards, who, knowing that his escape might bring the savages on them, kept a keen eye on his slumbers.

"To-morrow," said Jack, as they turned in, "we will return to Cuavaca for the troops, and before night-fall they shall camp in the ruined city."

CHAPTER XI.

THE DESTINY OF THE OPAL.

The spirit of fire,
The sylph of the air,
The gnome of the earth,
The dangerous wave-dwelling fay ;
All madly desire,
The opal-stone rare,
Which at its birth,
They gifted with rainbow hues gay.

Earth-gnome caressed it,
Sylph did enfold it,
Wave-nymph doth chain it,
In spite of the flame spirit's desire ;
Two have possessed it,
Now doth one hold it,
Yet will he gain it,
The terrible spirit of fire.

THERE were many Indians in Cuavaca, and had
these entertained any suspicion that there was a second
secret way to the sacred city by the cañon road, they
would have at once warned Ixtlilxochitli of the im-
pending danger to the Chalchuih Tlatonac. As it

was, however, they could not conceive the reason of the troops leaving Cuavaca for the interior of the country. From their wanderings in that district, they knew perfectly well that the line stopped suddenly in the midst of a dense forest, and there appeared to be no reason that soldiers should be sent thither. The generally received opinion among them was, that as the Indians of the north had been on the war-trail, these soldiers were sent up by the Government to punish such rebellion. With this idea, the peons of Cuavaca took no heed of the expedition, knowing that it would be impossible for civilised troops to discover their brethren in the vast forests among the rugged mountains.

Thus, when next day at noon the explorers returned to lead the soldiers to the buried city, none of the Indians suspected the truth. Indeed, the troops themselves were in absolute ignorance as to their destination, as Rafael, thinking the Indians of Cuavaca might learn too much, ordered the soldiers to blindly obey his orders, and not question as to where they were going. Thus he hoped to camp a thousand men that night within the streets of the ruined city, and surprise

Totatzine by dawn, when the priests and the populace would be engaged in worshipping the opal. The wall towards the cañon would be quite undefended, as never within the memory of the priests had anyone come into this city from that direction. Ixtlilxochitli thought that the way was quite blocked up, and never for a moment deemed that his bitterest foes would capture the city from the cañon road.

All that day the trains went back and forward between Cuavaca and the clearing, taking troops into the interior of the country. So soon as they arrived at the railway terminus, they were marched off through the woods to the buried city, and there ordered to camp for the night, or at least till such time as their leaders chose to guide them forward. By sunset a thousand well-armed, well-disciplined troops were bestowed in the ruined city of the Toltecs, within fifteen miles of the opal shrine, and yet not a soul, save the leaders, knew that this was the case.

The troops having been brought thus far, Rafael, as leader of the expedition, held a council of war as to the advisability of remaining there for the night, or pushing on to the narrow path of the cañon so as to

surprise the inhabitants of Totatzine by dawn. Jack
and Tim were strongly in favour of marching at once,
and as Philip afterwards came round to this opinion,
Rafael almost made up his mind to move forward without delay.

"From here to the cañon torrent it is mostly tunnels," urged Jack, persuasively; "so whether we go by
day or night it does not matter, as we must carry
torches. We can easily march along that road on the
plateau between the two tunnels, and when we enter
the last one, can arrive at the bed of the torrent about
midnight. Let us camp there with as many men as
possible, and then march along the narrow path at
the first glimpse of daylight. Thus we will be able to
assemble on the platform under the pierced wall while
the populace and priests are in the great square of
the teocalli. They will be unprepared, and we can
capture the city without almost a blow."

"But they will be equally unprepared during the
day," said Rafael, with some hesitation, "so why not
wait here till dawn?"

"They will not be unprepared during the day,"
replied Jack, decisively, "that pierced wall has people

on it occasionally. Sometimes they come out on to the platform overlooking the torrent. If these saw our soldiers coming two abreast along the narrow path they would give the alarm, and the defenders of the city could kill our advance guard and block up the road. Now, if we can get five or six hundred on to the platform by sunrise, they can keep the populace at bay until the rest of our men arrive, then the city will be easily taken."

"Only two men can walk abreast on the path?" asked Philip, dubiously.

"As a matter of fact, three can walk abreast, but it is safer with two. The path is cut out of the side of the cañon, and is very dangerous. It must be attempted by daylight. Nine miles of narrow path in the dark would end in our losing our men. Besides, who knows but what that infernal Ixtlilxochitli, to make things quite safe, may not have destroyed portions of the path?"

"If he's done that, there won't be much chance of our taking the city," said Tim, in disgust.

"True, Señor Corresponsal," replied Rafael, gravely; "all things considering, I think it will be

O 2

best to take Don Juan's advice, and march two or three hundred men to the torrent camping-ground to-night."

This plan being adopted, the council broke up at once. It was decided that Jack and Rafael should push on with three hundred men guided by Pepe. These were to camp at the entrance of the tunnel where it led to the narrow path by the torrent. At dawn the remaining seven hundred men, under the leadership of Philip, Tim, and Captain Martez, should follow, and by the time they arrived at the torrent camping-ground, the advance troop would have reached the platform under the pierced wall, which they could hold till the reinforcements arrived. As a matter of fact, Jack and Rafael hoped to have the full strength of their men on the platform and in the city before the inhabitants took the alarm ; but, in any event, three hundred could hold the narrow path entrance to the platform while the rear came up steadily. Having settled these important details, they all made a hearty meal, and, after bidding their friends an affectionate farewell, Jack and Rafael, with their little band, pushed forward.

The men now knew that their destination was Totatzinc, and so many rumours were current in Cholacaca over the amount of treasure concealed in this sacred city that they were madly desirous of getting to the town. Without hesitation they followed Don Rafael and the Englishman up the grand staircase, from the entrance whence all rubbish had been cleared away. On arriving at the top, they saw the broad paved road stretching straight before them in the semi-darkness, and still keeping their torches lighted to guide them on their way, marched steadily along the five miles until they arrived at the foot of the great peaks. Here was the shallow tunnel, also choked up by rubbish. This was speedily cleared away by a hundred willing hands, and then the leaders making Pepe go down into the darkness between his guards, followed with their men. The zambo made no attempt to escape, as now seeing the power of the Junta, and knowing that his life was safe, he had quite gone over to the side of Don Hypolito's enemies.

The staircase led downward into the bowels of the earth for over a quarter of a mile, then suddenly admitted them into a vast gallery through which the air blew keenly. Jack was unable to restrain his admiration at the mechanical skill which the Toltecs— if they had been the engineers—displayed in thus piercing these vast tunnels through the solid rock. The red glare of the torches showed them that the sides were cased in brick painted with images of the gods, and the path under their feet was smoothly paved with stonework, worn by the feet of countless generations. To accomplish such marvels, these long-dead nations must have possessed wonderful engineering capabilities, and employed thousands and thousands of slaves. The latter might have been taken in war, and forced to labour at these colossal works, but where the Toltecs learned engineering was more than Jack could discover.

The tunnel was only a mile long, and in a short space of time they emerged on to a vast natural platform at the very bottom of the cañon. To the left, looking from the tunnel, the great gap ended at the distance of a quarter of a mile, and through the opening they could see the flat extent of plains, and the distant pinnacles of mountains. On the right the cañon turned suddenly to one side, and they saw themselves shut in, so to speak, by vast rocky walls towering up to the height of some thousands of feet. The torrent gushed and raged a little distance below the natural terrace, and on one side of it arose a narrow flight of steps leading to the path which ended at the sacred city itself.

So difficult had been the way that it was now nearly midnight, so the wearied troops camped on the terrace, and made a meal as best they could. There was but little chance of their presence being discovered by any human being in that desolate cañon, but Rafael, judging it best to be on the safe side, forbade them to light fires. Fortunately the night was warm, every man possessed a zarape, and they slept in comparative comfort.

It was a critical period, as discovery by any wandering Indian meant death to the whole band in that narrow gulch ; but, to Rafael's relief, the dawn broke showing not a human being to be in sight. They saw the narrow path winding like a thread along the rocks in the distance, and it looked a dangerous way to go. It was, however, the only way to the city, and once they arrived under the pierced wall, they could keep the path open for their reinforcements to follow.

Jack made the men eat a hearty meal before starting, and would liked to have made them drink hot coffee, but that there was a risk in lighting fires. At the first faint light of morning, which was about six o'clock, the men having finished their meal, looked to their rifles and ammunition, flung their zarapes round their shoulders, and prepared to ascend the narrow staircase.

Still keeping Pepe before all as guide, lest he should send them forward into some unknown danger, the two young men mounted to the path, and in the space of an hour the whole company were winding along two abreast. Below they looked down thousands of feet, above the cliffs arose stern and precipitous, but the path, though narrow, was well-made and safe, so, two by two, they marched forward in silence.

"In a couple of hours the rest of the troops will reach the torrent," said Jack to Rafael, as they walked along; "and by the time we gain the pierced wall, they will not be far behind."

"Once we are on the platform you speak of, I do

not care, Juan," replied Rafael, grimly; "but I hope by all the saints the Indians will not see us before we can get off this path. They could cut us off with the greatest of ease."

"Never fear," said Duval, casting an anxious look at the sky, still cold and grey; "at sunrise they will all be in the great square worshipping the opal. Totatzine, you know, Rafael, is a sacred city, and it is death for any inhabitant to remain away from the morning sacrifice. That is how the priests keep their hold on the people."

"But the women?"

"They will be present also."

"It must be a large plaza," said Rafael, disbelievingly.

"Very large. Much larger than the Plaza de los Hombres Ilustres at Tlatonac."

"Dios! What clever people those Toltecs must have been."

As they proceeded, the cañon wound to right and left, shutting itself in at every curve with its own walls, so that they never saw more than a short distance before them. Jack feared lest the path should suddenly come to an end behind one of the curves ; but as Pepe, who knew the way, marched boldly on, this did not seem possible. The grey sky began to flash crimson, and the stars to the eastward died out in the rosy hues of dawn. They could see the torrent far below like a white thread, and hear its voice, hoarse and incessant, rising upward. The serrated summits of the cañon rocks loomed black against the changing sky.

On, on, and on. The road never seemed to come to an end, but stretched ever before them narrow and perilous-looking, a hanging-way between heaven and earth.

"I hope to the Lord none of the men will grow dizzy, and fall over," said Jack, anxiously ; " the path is so narrow, the depth so terrible."

"No fear of that, mi amigo," replied Rafael, cheerfully ; "they are all too determined to get gold and silver in Totatzine to lose the chance of not arriving there. Believe me, Juan, they are as anxious as we are to get to the end of this infernal path. By the way, Martez and Señor Felipe must be on it by now, with their men."

Jack glanced at his watch.

"Yes; we have been over two hours now, marching. I expect Martez will press onward as quickly as possible, so as to join us without delay. Hullo!"

"What is the matter?"

"I saw a glimpse of green just now. We are nearly at the end of the journey."

The word passed along the narrow line of men, and they grasped their rifles tighter, with fierce joy at the thought that they would soon be in the heart of the golden city, so famous throughout Cholacaca. The path began to slope downward gently. It turned round a corner sharply, and lo! before them, Jack and his friend saw the sacred town, sparkling like a jewel, in the hollow of the green valley. A wall, glistening like silver, stretched along the whole front of the cañon, and before this was a broad stone platform, on which a thousand men could assemble with ease. Below was the torrent, and on this side of the rocks was a narrow path, ending abruptly in a precipice. Jack pointed out this latter to Rafael.

"Do you see that, my friend?" he said, slowly; "it leads from the secret entrance to the other path below the bridge, in the centre of the town. If you took that way, you would fall into the torrent, and be lost for ever."

"Dios!" said Rafael, awestruck, "what devils are these priests."

The platform and wall were absolutely deserted. The gates were wide open, and through the vast archway they could see into the streets of the town. A rosy flame, with yellow shafts, appeared behind the arid peaks of the east, and loud and shrill the invaders heard the sacred hymn, saluting the rising luminary. For centuries that song had not been heard by the white man—not since Montezuma's altars had ceased to smoke had civilised beings seen what they now saw. A vast pyramid in the centre of the city, crowned with a silver temple, and dotted at the summit with tiny figures invoking the gods. It was the last time that song would ever rise; the last time the sun would be saluted with bleeding victims and rolling incense; for the last stronghold of the Aztec deities was discovered. The waves of advancing civilisation were about to roll over this primeval city, and blot it and its fierce deities out for ever.

Silently, with anxious hearts, the little band turning the last corner of the path, stepped downward on to the platform. When Jack found himself there, he breathed a sigh of relief. Even though the Indians found them now, they could not stop them in their onward course. His men poured on to the platform, fell into line silently, and thus established a defence at the mouth of the narrow path, while their comrades rapidly came onward to their assistance. The city was as good as won. But Xuarez——

"We must take care that Don Hypolito does not escape, Señor," said Rafael, anxiously, as the troops massed themselves under the pierced wall.

"Leave that to me, Rafael. I have an account to settle with Xuarez. He shall not escape me."

"Shall we attack the city at once?"

"I think so. It will be as well to get inside the walls, lest we should be discovered and the gates closed. Leave fifty men on the platform, mi amigo, so as to hold it open for the reinforcements, then we can penetrate into the town."

"Making for what point?"

"The great square. We must capture the bridges,

and so hold the people who are now worshipping on one side of the city. They shall thus not be able to get their weapons."

"The reinforcements will arrive shortly."

"In about an hour, I fancy. I told Martez to march as rapidly as possible, and I have no doubt he is pushing on with all speed. Come, then, Rafael! Let us march into the city, and don't forget to seize Xuarez and the opal! Also we must rescue Cocom."

"What about Ixtlilxochitli?"

"Oh, throw him into the torrent," said Jack, savagely; "he was going to offer me up to that infernal deity of his. I believe he is making a sacrifice now."

"Perhaps it's Xuarez."

"I hope so! We will be spared the trouble of shooting him."

By this time the full number of men had arrived on the terrace, and leaving fifty men to guard the path, Jack, in company with Rafael, pushed forward through the gate into the city. No sooner had they got inside, and were marching down the street leading to the principal bridge, than some women saw them.

Thunderstruck at their appearance, these paused, and then began to yell loudly. Rafael sent forward some soldiers to seize them, but they disappeared, running in the direction of the great square.

"Carajo!" muttered Maraquando, savagely; "they will alarm the town. Forward, men! Keep close together. Señor Duval, take fifty men, and hold the lower bridge. I, with one hundred, will keep the middle one, and you, Señor Riconada, can hold the bridge near the wall with the rest of our forces. Thus we will be able to keep all the Indians in the square till the arrival of our friends."

Jack and Riconada hastened to obey these orders and blockaded the three bridges. Scarcely had they established themselves when the serpent-skin drums on the summit of the teocalli began to roll out the alarm. Frantic with rage and astonishment, the worshippers streamed towards the three bridges so as to repel the daring foes. No one could understand how these invaders had entered the city, and Ixtlilxochitli smitten with fear, called on the children of Huitzilopochtli to defend their god. The crowd pouring towards the bridges were driven back by the soldiers, and as they were without weapons, owing to having gone to the square for sacrifical purposes, they could do nothing. Ixtlilxochitli was equal to the occasion, and from some secret store produced shields and spears, bows and arrows, and swords of obsidian. The drums rolled, the trumpets shrilled, and the priests on the platform of the teocalli frantically invoked the god, while those whom they had aroused desperately attempted to force the bridges.

A feeling of superstitious terror was in the breasts of the Indians. These terrible white men, whom no obstacle seemed to hinder, had entered Totatzine as though by magic. How they had evaded the spies and overcome the difficulties of the secret way none knew, much less how they had discovered the passage. No one thought of the cañon road, not even Ixtlilxo- chitli, who never dreamed of danger from that quarter. All the inhabitants of Totatzine knew was that their worst foes were in the heart of their sacred city, and that, unless they drove them forth at once, the Shrine of the Opal would be lost for ever.

Flights of arrows fell round the soldiers holding the three bridges, and many were killed, as they had no shields with which to protect themselves. On the other hand, the round bucklers held up by the savages were no hindrance to the bullets of the invaders, and as the soldiers kept up a steady fire into the dense mass of worshippers, the ground was soon cumbered with the dead and dying.

Jack in vain looked for Xuarez, but could see no sign of him. On the summit of the teocalli he saw a vast crowd of priests crying on the war-god to defend his shrine, and thought for a moment, as the black mass parted, that a man was lying on the stone of sacrifice. But the next instant the throng closed together again, and he was forced to give his attention to the task of defending the causeway. His soul revolted against this butchery, and he ordered his soldiers to deal as gently as possible with the comparatively defenceless enemy. Nevertheless, he knew that the safety of himself and his friends depended on keeping the Indians blockaded until the reinforcements arrived, and was forced to massacre the crowds which hurled themselves with fanatical devotion against his men.

Owing to the depth of the torrent, there was no way

of crossing it save by the bridges, and these being held by the invaders, it was impossible for the Indians to fight to any advantage. Wave after wave rolled across the narrow bridges, and midway were repelled by the incessant fire of the Tlatonacians. The spears and arrows of the Indians did deadly work, and the centre of the causeways were soon filled with corpses, white men and red men mingled promiscuously together. Jack saw plainly that the three bridges could be held by them for hours, yet wished from his soul that Martez and Philip would come up with the reinforcements, if only to put a stop to this wholesale massacre.

Thousands of Indians were pent up in the square of the sacrifice, all arrayed in festal robes of white with chaplets of flowers. These latter were now torn off and cast underfoot, the white garments were spotted with blood—the blood of their friends—and, frantic with rage, the multitude did all that valour could do to break through the handful of men holding the bridges. The drums were rolling their thunder incessantly, the trumpets shrieked like human beings, priests bellowed, the worshippers yelled, and constantly could be heard the ominous cracking of the rifles, as every shot carried death into the white mass heaving tumultuously in the square.

All at once a trumpet beyond the walls rang out clear and thin.

"Hurrah!" cried Jack, waving his sword, "the reinforcements at last."

It was indeed the seven hundred men, who had arrived sooner than was expected. Martez, anxious to aid his leader as speedily as possible, had marched his men rapidly along the narrow path, and now they were steadily streaming through the gate, making for the several bridges where the fight seemed hottest. As the priests were shouting down encouragements to the people below, Rafael decided to attack the teocalli, and stop this work. Once the shrine was taken, and it was possible the Indians might yield without further trouble, a thing he heartily desired, as, like Jack, he was weary of this massacre.

Tim and Martez stayed with Don Rafael, while Philip joined Jack, and Peter, who was quite warlike in appearance, went to the town bridge, where Riconada was fighting. At a given signal, all three bodies of soldiers commenced to converge towards a single point, that being the teocalli. The priests saw this manœuvre, and bellowed with fear. Many threw themselves down the steep sides of the pyramid, in vain offering themselves to the war-god in the hope that he would decree victory to their fellow-country-men. The women in the square were shrieking wildly, and hurling stones, wrenched from the houses, at the soldiers as they pushed the mass of men steadily before them. From the summit of the pyra-mid a cloud of incense rolled heavenward, and Ixtlilxochitli, in the red robe of sacrifice, stepped for-ward to the verge of the steps, holding up the opal in order to encourage his people.

A yell arose from friend and foe alike as they saw the glint of the stone, and the Indians closed resolutely round the base of the teocalli in a vain attempt to prevent the enemy from taking it by storm. All their valour and self-sacrifice was in vain. The three compact bodies of men pushed forward, shoulder to shoulder, through the white mass, leaving behind three several streaks of red and yellow, the uniformed bodies of their fellow-countrymen. Ixtlilxochitli saw these rivers of fierce soldiery converge towards the staircase of the teocalli, and yelling aloud to Huit-zilopochtli, flashed the opal incessantly in the sun.

"There is Xuarez!" panted Philip, in the ear of Jack, as they cut their way onward.

"Where?"

"By Ixtlilxochitli. That chap in red. He is bound. By Jove, Jack, I believe the old fiend meant to sacrifice him."

"Pity he didn't," retorted Jack, grimly; "look out Philip. Ah, there is Tim. Hurrah, Tim! See which of us will reach the staircase first."

Even in the midst of danger, Jack could not help joking, and Tim burst out laughing as he hurled his huge form by Rafael through the crowd.

All at once their mirth ended. At the foot of the teocalli they stumbled over a nude corpse with a ragged wound in the breast. It was the body of Cocom.

"He has been sacrified," cried Jack, fiercely. "Forward men! Avenge his death."

The advancing troops cheered loudly, and pressed steadily on towards the great pyramid.

The soldiers in the other part of the city had set fire to the dwellings, and already the flames were rising heavenward. Mad with rage, the Indians fought on doggedly, but could do nothing against the discipline of regular troops ; inch by inch they gave way before the line of steel pressed against their breasts. The invaders stepped over corpses on their way to the teocalli, and those lying on the ground not yet dead, twining their arms round the legs of their foes, strove to throw them. The noise was something deafening, and the whole square was one vast field of carnage.

Jack and Rafael, with their respective troops, reached the foot of the staircase at the same time, and began to climb up. The priests, frantic with terror, threw down huge stones, tore the tiles off the shrine, and hurled them viciously at their foes. The drum was still beating, the incense rolling, and high above the din could be heard the strident voice of the old high-priest calling on his gods.

"Jack! Rafael! keep your eye on Xuarez; he is free," replied Philip, as they fought their way upward.

Such, indeed, was the case. Don Hypolito had

managed to get his hands free, and was now struggling with Ixtlilxochitli. Why he did so, none of the
Englishmen could make out, unless it was to kill the
old man for trying to sacrifice him to Huitzilopochtli.
The attendant priests closed round the struggling
figures to help their head, and thus omitting to defend
the teocalli, in a few moments the assailants were on
the top.

Jack sprang up first on to the platform, closely followed by Tim. The crowd of priests rolled on either
side, rolled over the sides of the pyramid, falling into
the frantic mass below. Then they saw the design of
Xuarez.

"Catch him Tim ; he has the opal !"

Xuarez, with torn clothing and pale, blood-stained
face, stood against the shrine with the opal flashing
in one hand and a spear in the other. Jack dashed
forward to seize him, and Xuarez, with a yell of rage,
hurled the spear. In a second Tim had thrown himself between the weapon and Jack, receiving it full in
his breast. He fell back with a cry into Philip's arms,
and Jack, mad with anger at his friend's disaster, flung
himself forward on Xuarez. The rebel leader dashed

to one side, and threw himself over the smooth side of the pyramid, sliding downward on his back. Jack, with his revolver firmly grasped in his right hand, followed in the same way; but before he reached the ground a red mass shot rapidly past him.

" Ixtlilxochitli."

The rebel leader, holding the opal on high, dashed through the crowd of Indians, who opened a path before the sacred gem, followed closely by the red figure of the high priest. Jack saw the idea Xuarez had in his head. He was making for the secret way under the bridge, hoping to escape to the mountains with his booty. At once he followed the flying figures, but the crowd closed around him, and he had much to do to protect himself. Martez saw his danger and sent a body of soldiers to his assistance. In a few minutes, he was safe on the bridge surrounded by his friends. Xuarez and Ixtlilxochitli had disappeared through the secret entrance.

Determined to revenge the wound of Tim and secure the opal, Jack would have followed, when he heard a hundred voices on the platform beyond the pierced wall shout out the name of Xuarez. Wondering the reason of this, he darted up the street, followed by a few troops, and on gaining the platform, looked over to where the soldiers were pointing.

On the rocky ledge below, he saw two men struggling for the possession of the opal. Xuarez, hotly pursued by the old priest, had taken the wrong turning below the bridge, and they were now reeling on the verge of destruction. Nearer and nearer they came to the brink, then Xuarez, evidently seeing he was lost, threw the harlequin opal into the torrent. The great gem described a curve in the air, flashed rainbow hues in the sunlight, then dropped sheer into the boiling torrent below—lost for ever to the world. In another second, Ixtlilxochitli had forced Xuarez over the ledge, and the two men, locked in one another's arms, shared the fate of the gem.

Jack stood on the edge of the platform, looking in silent horror at the fate of the rebel leader, when he heard his name cried out loudly, and turned to see Peter hurrying towards him with a face of horror.

"Jack! Jack! Tim!"

"Tim!" echoed Jack, with a pang of fear, "is he wounded?"

" He is dead."

Jack waited to hear no more, but, followed by Peter, raced back to the teocalli. With the fall of the shrine had fallen the city, and Jack, crossing the square untouched, ran up the staircase rapidly. There, on the summit, supported in Philip's arms, with Philip's tears dropping on his dead face, lay Tim, merry-hearted Tim, whom they all loved so truly.

" Oh, Tim!" cried Jack, with a burst of anguish, and fell on his knees beside the dead body.

Below the tumult continued, the incense still rolled upward ; but the last sacrifice had taken place in the teocalli of Totatzine, and Tim was the victim.

CHAPTER XII.

FAREWELL, TLATONAC.

Let us sail eastward, where the sun
 Slow rises o'er the crimson wave,
Our western toils at last are done,
 And rest, for ever, rest we crave.

Oh, see the shore fades far away,
 A dim spot in the distant blue,
And eastward breaks the coming day
 Which bids our life-day dawn anew.

Old times are at an end,—our lives
 Have had their share of sighs and tears ;
Now, loyal friends, with loving wives,
 We hopeful look to coming years.

A CHEER arose from the crowd at the sea-gate, the warships dipped their flags in salutation, the guns thundered from the forts, and *The Bohemian* steamed slowly out of Tlatonac Harbour. At her mainmast fluttered the Union Jack, over her stern drooped the Opal flag, for the daughter and niece of His Excellency Don Miguel Maraquando were on board, on their way to England, with their husbands, Sir

Philip Cassim and Jack Duval. That same day had they been married by Padre Ignatius, and were now departing for the honeymoon, therefore did the guns thunder, the people cheer, the flags dip.

Six weeks had elapsed since the fall of Totatzine, since the death of poor Tim, and many events had taken place during that interval. When the teocalli was captured and the priests slain, the Indians, deprived at one blow of gods and leaders, yielded in despair to their conquerors. Don Hypolito dead, Cocom sacrificed, the opal lost, nothing more could be obtained from the town, so Rafael withdrew his troops by the cañon road, and returned to announce to the Junta that they need no more fear the restless ambition of Xuarez.

Poor Tim's body was taken back to Tlatonac by his sorrowing friends. For a long time they could scarcely believe that he was dead. Tim, who was so light-hearted and full of spirits ; but alas ! there was no doubt that he had died almost instantaneously on the platform of the teocalli. The spear, thrown with vigorous hate by Xuarez, and intended for the breast of Jack, had dealt a fatal wound, and Tim had but time to grasp Philip's hand in faint farewell before he passed away. The three survivors were wild with grief at this loss, so cruel, so unexpected, and reverentially carried the body of their old schoolfellow to the capital for burial. In view of Tim's services during the war, and the regard entertained for him by the Cholacacans one and all, the Junta decreed a public funeral to the remains; so Tim's body, with much pomp, was consigned to the vaults of the cathedral, amid the firing of cannon, the knolling of bells.

It was some weeks before the three Englishmen could recover sufficiently from this cruel blow to attend to necessary matters. Now that the country was at peace, and Don Hypolito slain, the President gave his hearty consent to the marriages of Dolores, Eulalia, and Carmencita. The weddings were very quietly celebrated, as neither Jack nor Philip felt inclined for revelry now that Tim was dead; and, indeed, so many of the Tlatonacians had lost relatives in the late war, that public festivities would have been out of place. Therefore the weddings were celebrated by Padre Ignatius in a very quiet fashion, and afterwards Jack and Philip, with their respective brides, departed for England in *The Bohemian*, while Don

Rafael and Carmencita went north to Acauhtzin in a warship.

It was Philip's intention to establish himself and Eulalia in his ancestral home in Kent, and live the useful life of a country gentleman, varied by occasional voyages in *The Bohemian.* He could not make up his mind to part with the yacht, nor did Eulalia wish him to do so, and having proved herself to be a capital sailor, she took as much interest in the boat as did Sir Philip himself. Eulalia, having been shut up all her life in Tlatonac, now showed a decided desire for rambling, so it seemed as though even marriage would not cure Philip of his gipsy proclivities. Still before such matters were decided upon, the baronet deemed it advisable to instal his Spanish wife in the family mansion, and introduce Lady Cassim to the country people.

As to Jack and Dolores, they were only paying a flying visit to the old country for a few weeks, as Duval had finally made up his mind to settle in Tlatonac, and become a naturalized citizen of that city. The life suited him; he was married to a native lady of the place, and, moreover, the Junta had given

him full control of all engineering works connected
with the country ; so Jack, with the full approval of
Peter and Philip, thought he could not do better than
establish himself in this new land. The country was
rich in natural productions, in timber, ores, and
precious stones, so when Jack's railways opened it
up throughout the whole length, there was no doubt
but that Cholacaca would become one of the most
flourishing Republics of the Americas.

Owing to the severe lesson at Totatzine, it was
anticipated that the Indians would be too cowed to
give the Government further trouble, and this proved
to be the case. The last stronghold of the old gods
had fallen, and the sacred city, which had been the
centre of incessant conspiracy against the Republic
was quite broken up. With the vanishing of the
opal, it lost its character of a sacred town, and now
being thrown open to the world by the discovery of
the secret paths, no longer possessed any mysterious
charm for the Indians. With no centre, with no
crafty priesthood, the power of the tribes, instead of
being concentrated, became scattered, and there is no
doubt that in the near future, when the country is a

network of railways, that the savage tribes will vanish
before the advancing flood of civilisation.

Peter did not come in *The Bohemian*, as he had
accepted the invitation of a celebrated naturalist to
visit him up Mexico way, and hunt beetles and
butterflies in company. Faithless Peter, he refused to
marry Doña Serafina, and fled the smiles of his
elderly charmer, for the, to him, dearer delights of
entomology. Baffled in one quarter, Doña Serafina
was successful in another, for she turned her attention
to Don Alfonso Cebrian, and succeeded, after some
difficulty, in marrying the Intendante of Xicotencatl,
who had for some years been a widower. Serafina
found on marriage that she possessed a step-daughter,
with whom she could not agree, but speedily settled
her future by marrying her off to Captain Velez, who
thus became the Intendante's son-in-law after all.

After leaving Tlatonac, the four people on board
The Bohemian were talking of these things on
deck, in the warm sunshine. It was the afternoon of
a perfect day, and the yacht steamed merrily along
towards the distant ocean. To the surprise of Philip
and Jack, the ladies proved to be excellent sailors,

and were quite fascinated with the yacht, much to the gratification of old Benker, who, for the first time in his crusty old life, approved of the existence of the female sex.

When they were tired roaming about and making inquiries about this, that, and the other thing, they settled down in comfortable deck-chairs to talk about the future with their respective husbands. Dolores and Jack were returning to Tlatonac shortly, so had but the same life to look forward to ; but Eulalia was secretly dismayed at the prospect of being an English lady.

" Querido! " she said to Philip, looking at him over the top of her big black fan, " I cannot talk your tongue. And your English ladies! I hear they are so cold. And your climate. Oh, Felipe, I fear your climate."

" Who told you all these nice things, Eulalia ? " asked Philip, smiling.

" Don Pedro."

" My dear girl, you must not believe what Peter says. He doesn't know a thing, except what relates to beetles. You are learning to talk English very quickly, and as to the English ladies—they will all fall in love with you."

"And the climate of England," added Jack, wickedly, "is the best in the world."

"No!" replied Philip, laughing, "I cannot conscientiously say that. But neither Eulalia nor myself will stay much in England. We shall travel."

Eulalia clapped her hands with glee on hearing this delightful proposal, and Dolores settled the future course of such travelling.

"Wherever you may go, Señor Felipe," she said smiling, "forget not that Juan and myself dwell in Tlatonac, and shall expect you both once a year."

"More or less!" cried Jack, lazily. "Come in a year, Philip, and you will see how Cholacaca is going ahead. I will have that railway to Acauhtzin ready before you know where you are. All those little forest towns will soon be in communication with the outside world—— "

"And Totatzine?"

"Ah, Totatzine has lost its mysterious charm of the unknown. I'll turn it into a resort for invalids, or a Central American Monte Carlo. Where Huitzilopochtli was worshipped, future generations will adore the goddess of play."

"At that rate, you will still have victims offered at the shrine," said Philip, grimly ; "but, after all, Jack, it was a pity we lost the opal."

"Can it not be found again?" asked Dolores, who deeply regretted the vanished jewel.

Jack shook his head.

"I am afraid not. Xuarez threw it into the torrent. Heaven only knows in what profound depths it now lies. Perhaps it is best so. While it was on earth, it caused nothing but trouble, from the time it was in the possession of Montezuma, to the death of Xuarez."

"Now it is lost, I suppose the superstition will die out!"

"Superstition dies hard. All kinds of legends will grow up about that famous gem. It will still be remembered for many years, the more especially as Tlatonac is still, and ever shall be, the City of the Opal."

"And Dolores is still the guardian of the opal," said Eulalia, pensively.

" A guardian of a stone that has now no existence,"
replied Dolores, laughing ; " but, after all, I had rather
the jewel was lost than my Juan."

" Ah, Dolores ! " said Jack, with a sad smile, " had it
not been for the Señor Corresponsal, your Juan would
have been lost."

" Poor Tim," muttered Philip, softly, turning away
to conceal his emotion.

The tears sprang to Dolores' eyes, and Eulalia was
scarcely less affected. It seemed too terrible that they
should all be so happy, when poor Tim, whom they
loved so much, should be lying in the grave. The
bitterest part of it was that the death had taken place
just when the war was over. Tim had escaped the
siege of Janjalla, the battle of Centeotl, only to fall in
a skirmish at the obscure town of Totatzine. It was
fate !

They remained silent for a few minutes, thinking of
the dead man, and then Philip aroused himself with
an effort.

" Come ! " he said, with a smile. " We must not be
melancholy on our wedding-day. Poor Tim himself
would have been the last to countenance such folly.

We can talk of other things. Of Rafael, for instance."

"There is not much to talk about Rafael," said his sister, lightly ; " he is married to Doña Carmencita. He is now Governor of Acauhtzin, and when Cholacaca has a fleet, he shall be its almirante. I think Rafael is very fortunate, Felipe."

"Not so fortunate as I am," replied the baronet looking at her fondly.

"Nor as I !" cried Jack, slipping his arm round Dolores' waist. "Ah, Philip, how many things have taken place since we sailed over these waters ! Did I not tell you you would bring home a bride ? "

"You did, and I half believed you. For once, you have prophesied correctly. I am grateful to you, Jack, for having led me to secure this prize. When you came back to England, I was settling down into a crusty old bachelor; but now you will find me a devoted husband—all through your coming to England."

"Say, rather, all through the agreement we made at Bedford School, so many years ago. That boyish freak has brought us good fortune and charming wives,"

"Yet Peter is still a bachelor."

"Oh, Peter will marry a beetle! I expect we shall see him in England shortly. For myself, I do not complain of Fate ; nor does Dolores."

Jack bent down tenderly, and kissed Dolores, which example seemed so good to Philip that he at once followed suit.

The sun was setting in the west, and the sky was one blaze of colours. Pale rose, tawny-yellow, and high above, the delicate blue of the departing day. The sky, the sea were all glittering with rainbow hues of unexampled brilliancy. The yacht, leaving all this splendour behind, steamed steadily onward towards the coming night.

"It is like the Chalchuih Tlatonac," said Dolores, pointing to the sunset.

"And we are leaving it behind," replied Jack, taking her hand ; "but I do not regret it, querida, If Fate has denied me the harlequin opal, she has given me a dearer and more precious gift—yourself."

THE END.

www.ingramcontent.com/pod-product-compliance
Lightning Source LLC
Chambersburg PA
CBHW030103030726
47498CB00007B/2228